MURDER

In The Morning

I paced the floor of the university president's suite. Mrs. Scott, his secretary, came out the door of his office. "Susan, would you come in, please?" she asked, her face ashen and her voice trembling.

My heart started to pound. He's already angry and he's taking it out on her, I thought. He's going to play *macho* today. I went inside.

President Barker was slumped over his desk, his arms spread wide. A heart attack, I thought. Then I saw the red skullcap over his shock of gray hair. Blood!

I noted the details. His eyes were open, his face slack in total surprise. Some sort of ebony sculpture lay on the blotter next to his head.

"I think I ought to call the police," Mrs. Scott said from near the doorway.

"Good idea," I said. "And I'll take that cup of coffee now, and you should have some, too." It was going to be a long day.

PRIME SUSPECT

R.D. Brown

A TOWER BOOK

Published by

Tower Publications, Inc.
Two Park Avenue
New York, N.Y. 10016

One

My first case was a dilly, but it didn't start that way. At the Saturday morning hearing, Naomi, my client, was sweet and demure in a dark shirtwaist dress, answering my questions in a quiet voice as patient and relentless as an electric sewing machine. By the time she'd finished her testimony, Cartwright's attorney was doodling, looking up only to glare at Cartwright. He passed the cross examination and said he had nothing to add to his client's filed depositions. Seven minutes later the committee returned to say they'd reached a verdict on Naomi Wilson in case number 81-001.

By eleven, I'd explained to Naomi that though this was the important step, we still had the president and the board to meet, but I did think she'd be reinstated with back pay—perhaps as soon as Monday, but certainly within the week. She looked at me, her handsome, dark face enigmatic, clearly not as happy as I was. Then I remembered that for a plaintiff, a victory in court only means winning what is deserved. A loss is a major miscarriage of justice. The winning advocate looks at it differently, of course. I felt unambiguously good. It was my first accomplishment as Benson's first, full-time, female Affirmative Action officer.

I was humming "Chantal" to myself as I put away the stenorette and began to change into a jogging outfit for my noon date with Kenny Sears, a Robert Redford look-alike who was Benson's part-time tennis and track coach. Then Arnold Lawnover, President Barker's administrative assistant, rang my phone and life at Benson started up like a runaway merry-go-round.

"Miss Meredith? Glad I caught you in on a Saturday morning. I thought I was the only one who worked Saturdays. I must see you immediately on a matter of considerable importance. Fifteen minutes. All right!"

It wasn't a question, it was an order. And it wasn't all right. But I was new to this campus, and that meant putting up with it because his boss wasn't going to like what I'd be telling him Monday morning, and he deserved some warning. Since I'm a second-generation college brat, I had a good idea why Lawnover called. He wanted to impress me—because I was new—with his total dedication to work, no matter the day and hour, as long as it inconvenienced me at no cost to himself. Three different people had warned me about him, but so far I'd only seen him at a distance at receptions and parties—a plump short man who looked as if he were made out of peanut butter. He always dressed in tweeds as if for a weekend at an English country house, but that was as sporting as he got.

Lawnover arrived five minutes late. Then he stood in the doorway and took in my jogging outfit as if it were a bikini, though I think it makes me look like a drab teddy bear, it's been washed so many times. He was the one who could stand some exercise, I thought. Much too plump for a man in his early thirties, he carried himself as if he were fifty, worn out by a long and distinguished career. In my book he was one of those unappetizing men who think they are irresistible as they are, no matter how they are.

Take his clothes. He thought he was an Ivy League dandy. This morning he was wearing a button-down checked shirt with a paisley print tie, a vest, coat, and pants of three different plaids, a handkerchief in his breast pocket, two-toned shoes with waffle soles, and one of those little leather boutonnieres. As you can see, I watch men, but this one made my eyes hurt with all those different patterns. He thought he was all set for a sporting afternoon—probably watching football on TV while his wife brought him beer. What effect there was was spoiled because his pants were two inches shy of his shoes, cuffless, and blanketed with the hair from a dog of some inferior breed. Daniel Derbyshire had spent a lot of time explaining men to me in terms of the way they wore their clothes.

He slipped the clip-on shades from his aviator glasses and tucked them away while he waited for me to applaud.

"Going jogging? That's fine," he announced. "Sound mind and great legs. Still a nifty combo, even in this age of female liberation. This shouldn't take too long, Susan." He put on a serious expression and settled into a chair as I started coming to a boil. "Sit down," he invited grandly as he pulled at his pants legs to preserve the creases. "Susan," he said again, "you're new here, and maybe you don't understand your role at Benson. I thought it only fair to give you some off-the-record advice."

I've been getting that kind of advice from men since I turned fourteen. Usually, it's on topics I understand perfectly well, but I've never gotten used to it. Lawnover stopped memorizing my knees and stared at the ceiling.

"Susan, we expect the Affirmative Action officer to *affirm* the policies of the university." He paused to make sure I understood.

"Those are my expectations, too," I told him. I don't like pompous jerks interfering with my jogging plans on Saturday.

"This Wilson case. It's been blown out of all proportion. We can't legislate morality. Men are going to look at women with lust in their hearts the way they always have, no matter what the libbers say or how many ERA laws are passed."

"I agree," I said, "but that's not the case here."

"Let me finish," he said abruptly, although he'd given me one more of those long intervals intended to give my tiny mind a chance to grapple with his deep concepts. He could make a saint moody with his pregnant pauses. Then he started in again. "Naomi Wilson is a troublemaker. I observed her on many occasions. She's quite a dish, and she dresses provocatively. Too tan for my taste, of course." He smiled doggishly and I felt like retching. "If a woman's whole behavior is provocative, why should she be troubled if someone calls her up and invites her out for a drink?"

Again, it wasn't a question, but a lot of answers popped into my head—most of them beginning with four-letter words. Even if I had replied, he was listening to the sacred sound of his own voice and it wouldn't have mattered. He probably heard Montovani strings when he spoke anyway. He went on as sisterly anger raced over my skin like a rash.

"Moreover, I'm sure you yourself, Susan, have encountered that kind of homage quite often. It is routine to one who is young, beautiful, and available."

That did it! His insults were for Naomi, but all women were his target. "Dr. Lawnover!" I said, standing up in a rush. "Are you accusing me of being a loose woman?"

That got to his poise all right.

"But, but, but," he began like a motorboat with water in the gas line, "I was referring to Ms. Wilson!"

"Perhaps we should play the tape of this conversation," I said, just to be mean, though there was no tape. I hate to be ogled by someone I don't like. "You made no mention of Naomi Wilson, you said *I* was available."

He began to sweat gently. I don't like putting people down, but Daniel taught me to protect myself, and that meant listening carefully to what people say. Besides, if every pretty girl is considered fair game, any kind of male behavior is acceptable. I had his attention, so I picked up my notes for the report on the case. I slapped it down on the table. My verbal karate attack seemed to have stunned him into silence.

"I will accept your apology for your perhaps inadvertent words," I said grandly. "Do you think, sir, that Ms. Wilson is available because she's black? That adds a dimension of racism to the sexism that is apparently rampant on this campus. She's a qualified secretary and lives with her maiden aunt. Her references are uniformly excellent. Her clothes," I went on, "are no more provocative than mine. But that's beside the point."

He was a slow learner. He broke in on me. "You can't seriously expect Benson to sacrifice a senior administrator who was merely exercising his first amendment rights of free speech for some little snip of a secretary. It's unjust!"

Lord and Aphra Behn! The Constitution yet! Next it would be the Magna Carta in defense of sexual harrassment. But he did it again, broke in on me.

"Surely you can't want to sacrifice a man of mature years, a senior administrator, to some little snip of a secretary! It's grotesque!"

We all have our perspectives, I reflected. Grotesque, indeed! "Two points, Dr. Lawnover. First, Mr. Cartwright admits making the advances. He denies only that the firing was related to her refusal. The fact is not in dispute. There is a good deal of circumstantial evidence to indicate his motives, enough so that a committee of faculty and staff were convinced. Second. Mr. Cartwright is not being sacrificed. My recommendation is that Naomi Wilson be reinstated, in another office, with back pay. If he is to be punished, that's up to President Barker."

"Oh, he'd never—" Lawnover began and then stopped abruptly. He pursed his lips and then sighed as if he had to rein himself in as he dealt with a backward child.

"Susie, how old are you?"

Bringing him along slow wasn't working. I was certain he was at least ten years older than I, but I think I've had more experience of the world. At least I could teach him some manners.

"I'll tell you, Arnie, baby, when you tell me what size jock you wear. It's just as irrelevant. The law is the law."

He flushed and attempted a smile. I take that diminutive first name business just so long. It was six minutes to twelve. I stood up and looked down at him. He put on the expression of a man who finds a rock in his cream puff. Then he looked grave.

He steepled his fingers at me like a banker calling in a mortgage. "All this is beside the point, Miss Meredith. Our policy at Benson is to grant our chairmen and division heads considerable latitude in dealing with underlings. I happen to know what your recommendation will be, and I must tell you that it will not be welcome."

He got to his feet as if terminating the interview. I decided to become the little woman. I put on an expression of total puzzlement. It worked. Even as I spoke, his features began to plump up. "What I don't understand, Dr. Lawnover, is how you found out about the committee's decision before I reported it."

I swear that grease started to ooze from his pores. At

last, I had found my place. He gave me that patronizing look he had patented. "A college has many ways of communicating outside formal lines, Susan. That's why I came to you in all friendliness. It would create a difficult personnel situation if an employee could vanquish a superior. Discipline would be destroyed."

The patriarchal culture all the way! He spoke as if he were Moses reciting the tables of the law. "The alternative," I asked him sweetly, "is to destroy the Affirmative Action program?"

His superior look melted. "You have the weekend to rethink your report. I must say that I did not expect this attitude from the daughter of Daniel Derbyshire Meredith," he said, stressing the three names. He went on inexorably. "Perhaps you did not inherit your father's views. We should have investigated further before hiring you. It seems obvious, though, that the daughter of the country's leading conservative would disapprove of government interference in private affairs."

He was a fool. I decided to let him know I knew it.

"Who's this *we* you're quoting, Dr. Lawnover?"

"Benson University," he said as if that explained everything.

"I don't think so," I told him. "Are you saying you speak for the president in this matter?" I pulled a legal pad on a clipboard over and picked up a pencil, ready for dictation.

Lawnover's eyes swam around the fishbowls of his aviator glasses like desperate goldfish and I knew I had him. "Some—umm—matters of delicacy are best not committed to paper, as I'm sure you know," he told me.

"I agree. That's why I'm not going to write this up right now," I said. I made a big production of putting the pencil down. "I know that being a presidential assistant isn't always pleasant, Arnold. Either you're a glorified errand boy, or you pretend to make policy till something goes wrong. Then, you're expendable."

Lawnover's mouth came open gratifyingly. Susie, indeed! I went on to make sure Lawnover got the message. "Either you came to me on your own hook because you think President Barker wants an Affirmative Action program that means nothing, or he sent you. If he sent you and I raise a fuss, he can deny everything and say you exceeded your authority. In either case, you're out of a job!"

He turned pale. It was noon, straight up. I began to sort through the papers on my desk. "We both," I began majestically, "have tomorrow to decide what to do next. I have an appointment to see the president first thing Monday morning. You can decide what your move is in the meantime."

Lawnover swallowed a couple of times and stared at my now empty desk. He got the message that he'd made a serious mistake. After he turned to go, he stopped with his hand on the door knob to glare at me as if I'd kicked him hard in the shins.

"Faculty brat!" he spat and then he went out, slamming the door.

I sat down. My pulse was racing and tears of anger filled my eyes and slowly began to spill over and run down my cheeks. My first encounter with a chauvinist on this campus and I had gotten into a fight, taken off my velvet gloves, and now I was crying! It wasn't Lawnover, but what he'd said. Had they hired me just because I was Daniel Derbyshire Meredith's daughter? There was half a continent between us and I'd never mentioned the relationship. There are thousands of Merediths in every telephone directory. I wrote Diane Sampson's name on my calendar for Monday afternoon. She'd tell me if the campus had had any knowledge about me beyond my professional *vita.*

"Damn you, Daniel!" I said to my reflection in the mirror. Then I collected my gear bag and ran for the fieldhouse. I was going to get my exercise, no matter what!

The campus clock struck eight as I was drying my hair. It was Saturday night, and my big event was a shampoo after dinner alone—a green salad with anchovies and pimentos and rye bread croutons. I damned Daniel again. No matter where I was, he was exerting an influence on me. When it wasn't people responding to me as his daughter, it was people—men, usually—seeing me only as a piece of French pastry. I dropped the towel and looked at the packaging in the full-length mirror on the back of the bathroom door.

My best feature I got from my mother—a skin that never tans darker than a light toast color and remains smooth no matter how much I'm out in the sun. The sun in this southern city had started streaking my light brown hair blonde, but since I keep my hair fairly short, it doesn't look overly dramatic—just nice. Dale, the crazy poet, said my eyes were the color of root beer, and although he said a lot of other things were were clearly overstatements, I think he was right about the eyes. For the rest, I'm in good shape. Exercise keeps everything in proportion, and Cooper's Droop seems to be at least thirty years in the future. All in all, not bad, not bad at all—so why was I alone on a Saturday night?

It was Daniel's fault, but in a complicated way. He and my mother never married. At first I blamed her, but as I grew older and took a more intricate view of things, I changed my mind. No, it wasn't a tragedy of wartime, or an affair of star-crossed lovers kept apart by family or nationality or anything like that. If it was anything, it was ideology. My mother came from a family that also didn't believe in marriage, and hadn't for over six generations—since the French Revolution, in fact.

I heard the story for the first time when I asked why I didn't have a mother and all the other children in my nursery school did. I heard it again at intervals until I was fourteen, when I got the final version. Daniel and Miranda had met when he was on an overseas resident fellowship in Greece. She was the daughter of a French diplomat, a widower, the story went. They fell in love—Daniel still looks dashing, an Errol Flynn who's kept his looks—and Miranda, from Daniel's accounts was beautiful, intelligent, and accomplished. And something of an ideologue. He asked her to marry him and she said no. Not because he was poor or without prospects, and not because her father forbade it. The poor diplomat would have loved to have Miranda marry Daniel because he had been in the same situation as Daniel himself. He had loved a beautiful and exciting woman who refused to marry him but had chosen him to father a child—preferably female. Daniel heard it first from Miranda and then from her father. They were always named Miranda—if boys, the name didn't matter and the mother went off to find another man—but the crypto-Bourbon line was to be traced through the female *and it was not to die out!* One day, when the Bourbons were returned to the throne of France, the cadet line would be ready.

Naturally, Daniel thought he had gotten involved with a certifiable lunatic, lovely as she was. That had been the origin of the tradition, but his Miranda, *my* Miranda, used it only as an excuse. In the generations since the embittered *marquise* had begun the tradition, the women involved had created their own mystique, one that involved a rigorous critique of marriage. "Marriage is good for a man, but divorce is good for a woman," and "In marriage, man and woman become one person—the man,'' these and other one-liners were what Miranda regaled him with before, after, and during bouts in bed. Finally, as the price for continuing the relationship, Daniel agreed. That was when Miranda became pregnant. After she delivered me, she left Daniel, her father, and Greece. Where she had gone, he never learned. But he had me.

He certainly filled his part of the bargain. He told me the story early and often. Although he disagreed with the sentiment, he made sure I understood my mother's motives—and then proceeded to talk against them. Nevertheless, he didn't want me to waste myself on someone unworthy just so he could be surrounded by grandchildren in his old age, so he came up with a diabolical plan. From the age of eight, I began my lessons. Dancing, skating, skiing, swimming, fencing, tennis, and golf. At ten, singing, French, Italian, and drawing were added. From twelve on, I spent two hours a day with him and we discussed topics in economics, politics, and ethics. After I got into high school, we spent hours watching old movies from his collection while Daniel used the occasion to comment on life, the world, and men and women.

I didn't understand what he was doing until I got to college. At first I thought he was merely educating me so he'd have someone to talk to. A person as bright and knowledgeable as Daniel has trouble finding fellow conversationalists. But it wasn't that. His scheme was to make me so formidable that it would scare off incompetent men who can't abide women who excel in some fashion. It worked.

After the usual missteps with the usual types—*macho* rodeo types and a rebound to a druggic relict of the late sixties who said he was a poet, I settled down to my own pattern, which I guess, is like Miranda's. I have a lot of male friends, but each of them occupies only a part of my time. I'd been at Benson a little over a month, but already I had an advertising man I would ski with when the snow came, a lawyer who was a fantastic dancer I toured discos with, a doctor I took dutch to foreign films, and now—because Kenny Sears, the part-time coach, talked exclusively about macrobiotic nutrition—I had a jogging companion. I have one other recreation, but I haven't found an appropriate partner for it—yet.

I picked up the towel and buried my head in it after one last glance at the mirror with my lungs fully expanded. I exhaled and decided to think of something else, like seminal work in personnel administration, for example.

That fool Lawnover! No way did my *vita* show Daniel as my father. I wrapped the towel under my arms and padded into the living room of my University Tower efficiency to make sure. There I was. Susan M. Meredith, AB, Goucher; MA, Cal-Berkeley; Experience: VISTA; Legislative Intern, US Congress; Dean of Students, Hobatt College, Istanbul, Turkey. Three publications and a contract for a book on computer applications to personnel work. Not a hint about Daniel!

Then I figured it out. The word had turned up after I came to campus. As Daniel always says, American higher education is a village. He can step onto any campus in the country and meet someone he knows or a friend of someone who knows him. Probably it was chatter in an airport. "Charley, saw in the *Chronicle* that Dan Meredith's daughter is your new AA. If she's at all like her old man—" and no one, but *no* one, loves gossip like academics.

It wasn't really Daniel's fault. After I was born, he resigned his fellowship and came back to the states. He decided that California was a good place to raise child-dren—this was southern California before the great immigration began—and took a job at a college that had a Far East collection. He made himself an expert on temple ornamentation of the Ganges flood plain during the fourteenth and fifteenth centuries. Then a grant from the Etchver Foundation helped him bring out a book of color reproductions of the temple pictures and statues. Most of them dealt with explicit human manifestations of Krishna as Creator. Probably because Daniel spent a lot of time remembering Miranda, too. Anyway, the work had an immediate success at seventy-five dollars the copy. It went through eight impressions and then sold for the highest price ever paid for a nonfiction paperback. It was art to him but high-class porn to everyone else. The money rolled in. It was the only time I've ever seen Daniel discomposed. He didn't know what to do, so he began to get rid of the money by redistributing it to foundations in India, scholarly societies, to any place that would take it. He did this without the advice of a tax lawyer. When the IRS troops began to arrive, he saw that he was in trouble.

And that's how he became famous. He wrote *The Unnatural Act* in three weeks. It had everything—love and money, taxation and death, and the audience was ready. Daniel was considered an expert on sex, and everyone knew he was an instant millionaire, and now he was attacking the federal bureaucrats who were trying to take *his* money away from him. He was scathing, wrong-headed, bitter, brilliant—and writing what eighty-three percent of the taxpayers in the country thought but hadn't yet said.

The critics hailed him as a principled conservative, a political philosopher, and a wise man. Actually, Daniel's an anarchist, as I've told him many times. With the money from his *Unnatural Act,* he retired from teaching and invested hugely in tax exempts. Now he lives in a compound on Cape Cod where he is working on an encyclopedia of jade.

Daniel had solved all his problems, but I still had some because Lawnover's remark continued to fester. How tough had the competition for this job been? The whole process had seemed pretty casual, so that I thought at the time they'd already made up their minds and were going through a routine to keep out of trouble with Equal Opportunity.

Certainly, the interview schedule had been chaotic, with a number of people not being available for interviews. When I finally met President Barker, I was certain I was off-campus window dressing. He fidgeted all the time we talked, and the only question he asked was if I'd had a nice trip out. I had a lot of questions, but to them he offered only vague answers. Finally, he stood to pick up a golf putter. I thought the interview was over, and it was. He asked me if I wanted the job. When I said yes, he told me to see Bronterre to negotiate the salary details. He sighted down the shaft of the putter and said that he had found the secret of administration to lie in delegation and that I should remember that. Since my position involved me and one secretary, I said I'd work on it.

It looked as if I'd been hired as a result of some kind of special arrangement. I decided to make sure that no one they hired could do a better job than I would, so I was going to spend Saturday night going over all the files I hadn't yet seen. There was plenty about Benson I didn't know, and the best way to see where an institution is going, to quote Daniel again, is to read memos and find out where it's been.

There'd be nobody in the building, so I could wear casual clothes—blue jeans and a turtleneck sweatshirt. I was just going out the door when the phone rang. At eight-thirty, it wasn't going to be someone calling for a date, but I was going through the list of possible people I knew here when I picked it up. I knew it wouldn't be Daniel. He's never called me since I left home for college. I was thinking about him though, so it took me a moment to pick up on the voice that was coming over the wire.

"Drop. The. Case. Now. Or. You. Will. Regret. It."

Then it started over again at the same mechanical pace. It was a recording. I listened a second time and then hung up.

There had been a lot of signals, of which Arnold Lawnover's little presentation this morning was only the latest, telling me to lose the Wilson case in the files, but this was the message direct. Well! It wouldn't work, I said to myself in the wall mirror. Just the same, it had an effect. It had startled me, but no anonymous heavy-breather was going to stop me with a telephone message! Then I started thinking. Whoever it was had tried to disguise his voice, so it was someone I might recognize. On a sudden impulse I opened the directory and dialed Lawnover's home phone number without stopping to think.

Fortunately, it rang six times and I could with good grace hang up. I hadn't the slightest idea what I would have said—"Did you just make an anonymous phone call to me, you horrid person?" Then I wondered if it was really smart for me to go to an empty campus after this kind of a threat. I settled that by going out my door and punching up the elevator before thinking further. I reminded myself as I do when it's a choice between taking action or being passive that I was the granddaughter of a woman who had had Susan B. Anthony as a godmother. Then I encouraged myself with a Famous Female First. Did you know that the first novel in English was written by a woman, Aphra Behn? Now you do, I told myself sternly.

Benson Main, the oldest building on campus, housed the top administration, some of the smaller departments, and, so the rumor went, the service groups the president wanted to keep an eye on. Just the same, on Saturday night, it looked like a mood shot for a horror movie laid in the Old South. It was empty, and a greenish gloom from the Exit signs inside made the windows look like zombie eyes.

My key opened the main door and I hit the light switch just inside and dispelled all the shadows that would have frightened anybody not raised by Daniel and his stories about my mother. I was halfway up the first flight of stairs when the corridor lights expired. It was dark! Mary Wollstonecraft Godwin! I told myself, calling up the mother of the mother of Frankenstein to remind myself of my responsibilities. Then it came to me. The physical plant! In a gesture toward power conservation, they had installed minutiere lights for after-hours use. They were on for thirty seconds and then cut off automatically. The switchplates were phosphorescent and placed at the head of each flight. I'd seen a memo on the subject. I made the top of the first flight and hit the button. That phone call had gotten to me!

I climbed the rest of the flights at a jog, vexed with myself for being so nervous. Nevertheless, I was glad when I turned on all the lights in my office, a walled-in alcove between the philosophy department and student employment. It wasn't big, and there was no rug on the floor, but I had a reception area with an array of gray file cases and a private office a little larger than a phone booth behind them, a hint about the priority that Affirmative Action had on this campus.

As usual, the office was airless, so I propped open

both doors and threw up the window on the quad before going to work. I began with file one and worked through an amateur filing system that obscured rather than revealed information, as if a very clever filing clerk had tried to lose materials in plain sight.

It was eleven o'clock when I found what I hadn't known I was looking for. The official cover of the Title IX report had been torn off and the booklet was filed under "Miscellaneous," which was the largest file in the office. It was Benson's copy of the Compliance Review, signed by President Barker and the chairman of the Board of Trustees, a man named Simmonds.

I skipped to the Recommendations. I'm not interested in horror stories for their own sake. The first recommendation jumped out of the text: "The use of the presidential assistant as the Affirmative Action officer casts a chill upon potential grievants . . . It is recommended . . . a national search . . . candidates experienced in personnel work . . . with whom grievants can perceive a professional concern."

I asked myself what I was doing in such a snake pit.

"What are you doing here?"

I jumped.

A middle-aged man with a blue shirt stood in the doorway, a flashlight in one hand and his paunch resting on his belt. He needed a shave. Jogging was supposed to calm your nerves, I reminded myself. He was a campus security officer.

"I work here. I'm Susan Meredith, the new Affirmative Action officer."

Like most men, this one smiled when I smiled at him, revealing four front gold teeth.

"Saw your light, lady, and the open window. Both are violations of our security manual. I guess I've seen you around, but you don't look much older than an undergraduate, prettier, though. We have a rule this building shuts down absolutely at midnight. No exceptions, even for pretty girls."

I gave him my message received but no encouragement smile and said I'd be going in a few minutes and yes, I'd close the windows and he left. I made a few last pencil notes on my legal tablet. I'd put in a dismal three hours of reading cases that sounded like abolitionist literature just before the Civil War. Case after case that looked legitimate had been dropped, put in a pending file, or dismissed on what seemed pretty shaky grounds. I listened to the watchman's steps fade away and gathered up my notes about the people I wanted to talk to next week. By the time the big front door slammed, I was ready to call it a night. So Lawnover had been the previous AA officer. With a company fink like him in charge, no wonder they'd had a Title IX review, I thought as I closed the windows, put out the lights, and groped my way to the head of the stairs where the phosphorescent switchplate glowed an evil greenish white.

Just as I reached toward it, my wrist was grabbed and then another hand grabbed my forearm and someone tried to throw me downstairs! I punched out instinctively and then went limp. Whoever it was shifted grip and swung me around to slam me hard against the wall.

Emmaline Pankhurst! I thought, now somebody wants to rape me! I should have left with the security man, I told myself just before the thought came to me that he was the attacker. I must have driven him mad with my jeans and sweatshirt that read Stolen from the US Army across the front. I remembered his unshaven face and the gold teeth. We were pulling at each other, he to slam me against the wall again, and me to get away. Then I stopped thinking and began reacting. Singing and dancing, that was the way. I kicked out as if

I were doing *barre* exercises. One of my flailing feet caught something soft because I heard a harshly indrawn breath. Don't let him get close! a voice inside my head told me. Keep him at a distance! Thank goodness I was wearing joggers and jeans. His hand reached out to cover my mouth. Oh, yes, singing. I bit down hard on it and then I *screamed* when his hand jerked away. Actually, I sang because that projects better. I tried for E above high C. The people in the Music Department would say it was probably E flat, but I made noise.

"E-e-e-e-e-e-e-e!" I sang with a terrible taste in my mouth. I continued to flail and sing as I thought it over, trying to get loose from him. He was wearing rubber gloves! That scared me. It was someone who had come prepared. I stiffened my fingers and began to jab in the direction he seemed to be coming from. If I could poke a finger in his eye. Oh, why did women stop carrying hatpins? I broke loose and heard him breathing in heavy rasps. I could just make out a rectangle of night sky that was the window by the stairhead. Then a vague shape obscured the greenish-white of the switchplate and moved against the window—a sick-looking lump, like something in a nightmare. It came slowly at me as I continued to revolve my stiff hands and shriek in a voice that had become falsetto.

I moved toward the other wall, hoping I could jump past him. Once I thought he said *Shhhhhhh*, so I redoubled my noise. At least, he hadn't tried to tackle me. That would have ended the thing right there. Instead, he kept grabbing ineffectually at my swinging arms. I didn't know how this was going to end, but I did know that if he got me down, he was going to find I was all knees, elbows, fingernails, and sharp parts. Thank goodness for ballet lessons, I decided. This man didn't know his business. He grabbed me again, just as I was feeling I might get away, but I managed a kick where his legs joined his torso and he grunted like an animal. I decided to run at him, kicking as I went. That might change things.

It did. He closed in and shouldered me against the wall, where a fire extinguisher clattered in its holder as I was jammed against it.

I bit down hard on his thumb where it was creeping toward my throat. Then I grabbed the fire extinguisher and started to swing it at him.

MISTAKE!

Suddenly he had hold of the extinguisher and had caught my other arm. I managed to hit the release lever and swing the nozzle toward him. Immediately, he was what he'd been all along but more so. The flourescent foam made him into the Beast in White. Five seconds later, the extinguisher was empty and he had pulled it away from me and tossed it over his shoulder. That was when I had the only piece of luck that came my way that night. It went through the landing window with the sound of ice breaking. I started to run while he tried to get the foam out of his eyes, but I slipped in the mess I'd released and was falling even as he put a backhand blow across my face. I was suddenly on the floor and the back of my head hit a stair tread with a crack!

I didn't pass out, but a noise like Niagara filled my ears while I tried to get up.

Then the lights were on, and I heard someone huffing up the stairs. It was the old security man, and he was pretty angry, holding his flashlight like a weapon while his breath wracked his body. "You like to brained me with that extinguisher! What you still doing here anyway?"

He was going in and out of focus, but I could see he hadn't been my attacker. Then I heard a distant door slam.

"Somebody jumped at me. While I was trying to fight him off, I grabbed the extinguisher and shot it at him, but he threw it away, out the window."

The patrolman relaxed. "That door was him," he said sagely. "I been telling them about those fire doors for years. No way can you have security when people can get out of a building. They keep telling me it's state fire laws, but I think a comm'nist plot's what I think. Did you get a good look at him?"

He was an old man, waiting for his pension with nothing but the editorial pages of the newspaper to structure his world. I sat up and he offered a hand. Once on my feet, I didn't feel too bad. It was like being thrown from a horse the first time, everything happening so fast that when it's over, you find you've forgotten parts of it.

"You put up quite a fight, missy."

I had. I'd jammed one of my fingers where I'd missed him and hit the wall. A lump was swelling on the back of my head like bread rising, and my nose hurt where he'd backhanded me.

"I hate to see that starting again," he said. Mike read the badge on his shirt. "It's been three, maybe four years now since we had rapes on this campus. You want some transportation home?" He asked, taking my arm.

I know that a sexual attack is supposed to cool you off on men at some deep instinctive level, but I didn't feel that way—and I wasn't sure why. I patted his hand. He looked like a comfortable old great uncle. He acted as if rapes were an epidemic that came and went with sunspots.

"I'd like you to walk me to my car. How's that?"

That was fine. He kept a hand on my arm the whole way to my MG and then stood there watching as I drove off. I tried to figure out what was troubling me, but I couldn't. It was something about the attack—which I certainly hadn't encouraged. I didn't think I had any secret admirers who had ideas about me. That couldn't have been Kenny Sears tonight, for example. He could have flattened me immediately, and besides, I'd have recognized the smell of his perspiration. After all, a turtle neck and jeans on top of running shoes is *not* a provocative costume.

When I got home, I looked in all the closets, checked the lock on the door twice, had a drink of warm milk and decided I'd go to sleep and let my unconscious work out how to tell me what it was trying to say. I went right to sleep.

Two

I woke up Sunday, feeling as if I'd been in an auto wreck, so I stayed in bed for a while and thought. My unconscious finally came through. The attack on me the night before hadn't been sexual. It had been a case of simple assault. Then I remembered what had troubled me about the Wilson case from my first interview with Cartwright. Although he admitted propositioning Naomi, pleading an overpowering yen for her body, I had found that hard to believe. He was deep in his late middle age, and, frankly, he didn't seem interested in sex. But that didn't change the case in any way, so I spent Sunday afternoon reading the rest of the Affirmative Action files in my office. I left the building while the sun was still high in the sky. The bump on my head had gone down, but I decided I didn't need that kind of exercise again. I spent the evening pacing my living room, putting together my arguments for the meeting with President Barker the next morning. I went to bed about eleven, and I was still tossing and turning when the phone rang. I wasn't interested in any more anonymous calls, so I pulled the jack out of the wall and willed myself to sleep.

Monday morning was a beautiful late September day, a few high clouds and the sky a hard blue, making everything look sharp-edged, like my position on the Naomi Wilson case. I climbed the stairs to my office and went past the scene of Saturday night's attack. Two men from the physical plant were replacing the window. Another fire extinguisher was already on the wall. In a few minutes, there would be no evidence that anything had happened. That was fine with me.

When I walked into my office, Gloria Keeney, my secretary, looked up from the phone and showed me her teeth. She seemed to be on the phone all the time when she wasn't polishing her nails or admiring her coiffure, which changed every week. She was in her early thirties and obviously thought I was too young for the position I held. I'd warned her about discussing cases and she hadn't liked that. Apparently she didn't mind it enough to put in for a transfer, a fact I found puzzling till that minute. I wondered if she'd been the leak to Lawnover.

She put down the phone and looked critically at my tweed pants suit. "In the nick of time," she said. "Mrs. Scott called earlier to remind you of your nine o'clock with President Barker. I had to tell her you weren't in yet."

The wall clock read eight-ten.

"In that case you can call and confirm that I have finally arrived," I said as I walked into my office. Gloria was a divorcee taking courses in the Education Continuation Project toward a degree in sociology. She said her grades were straight A's, but I knew she'd drop out immediately if a man—any man—offered her marriage. She was a sister, but some sisters are a royal pain.

I sat down and stared at the Wilson case folder on the middle of my blotter. "Never have a confrontation needlessly." I could hear Daniel Derbyshire talking a half continent away. I picked up the phone and found Cartwright's number in the staff directory. He wasn't in his office yet, so I tried his home. Gloria picked up the phone as I was dialing the second time.

"I'm using the phone, Gloria," I told her, but it took

her a while to hang up. When Cartwright came on the line, I had my arguments ready. I asked if the resolution proposed by the committee was acceptable. At first, he seemed agreeable, but then he said he wanted to think a minute and put his hand over the receiver. I could tell he was talking to someone. When he came back on the line, he'd changed his mind.

"Nope. That little broad stays fired. I don't want her anyplace on this campus. That's final."

I thanked him and made a face at the phone. So much for accommodation. It was full speed ahead. Guiltily, I realized that I was looking forward to getting justice for Naomi Wilson. Daniel always said I had a contentious nature only slightly modified by my mother's sweetness and his reasonableness. Hah! Anytime Daniel Derbyshire Meredith was reasonable . . .

After that, I wasn't about to sit still. It was eight-thirty and I had half an hour to kill. I decided to walk around the academic quad to work off some of my excess energy. When I went through my reception area, Gloria was nowhere to be seen. She spent a lot of time drinking coffee with other secretaries, but she managed to get my typing done in good time, so I didn't fuss. I left her a note saying I'd go straight to my nine o'clock appointment and ran down the stairs.

Benson's academic quad was large, almost a quarter of a mile on a side, and at this hour almost deserted. Students with eight o'clocks were in class, and the nine o'clock scholars hadn't arrived on campus yet, so I had the place to myself. In this arid high country, the quad was an oasis. A long time back someone had planted all sorts of trees from all over the country and I tested my ability to identify them as I walked briskly along. When I looked at my watch, it was ten minutes to nine and if I didn't hurry, I'd be late for my hassle with the president.

I took a shortcut across the lawns and came up behind the administration building intending to run up the service ramp and go in the back way. I slowed down so I wouldn't arrive out of breath and began taking deep breaths to compose myself.

Mostly by chance, I happened to look up the ramp. As I did so, a physical plant delivery truck started down. I stared into the windshield because I didn't hear the enginc. I remember thinking that maybe its battery was down. Then I realized with a start that there was no one in the driver's seat and I had a real adrenalin rush.

The ramp was about two feet wider than the truck, one side was a high concrete retaining wall and the other was a drop-off onto a terrace that was mounded high with mulch for the winter. The truck was picking up speed and I remember thinking that if I jumped over the side I wouldn't hurt anything except my dignity but I'd be in no condition for the interview with President Barker.

About ten feet ahead I noticed a flight of stairs coming out of the retaining wall and I *ran*. I made it onto the first step when the car crashed into the retaining wall and scraped with a hideous sound of rending metal toward and then past me and then all the way down the ramp to end with a heavy screech-crump against a metal pylon at the bottom.

I stared at the truck and told myself some things. Chiefly that I had risked my life to avoid looking silly and/or missing an appointment with the president. It was five till nine. I better hurry, I told myself. Thank goodness I wasn't wearing heels!

It was two till nine when I pushed open the heavy leather-padded door to the president's suite. Mrs. Scott smiled encouragingly over her typewriter at me. The entire secretarial staff knew what we'd be discussing.

"It will be a few minutes, Ms. Meredith. Would you like coffee?"

I smiled my no thanks and began to walk back and forth while I studied the random design in the carpet. So, an accident almost wiped me out, but it hadn't and now I had an important meeting. I'll worry about that later, I told myself. Now let's get it together for the president. I don't want to have to threaten to resign to make something happen on this case, but that has to be an alternative. After all, Cartwright is one of Barker's people, brought in by him, so what's been going on will be no secret. I was starting to prejudge Barker's response despite all my training. That damned truck! If I were the scarey sort, I'd have thought somebody was out to get me. Then I remembered the attack Saturday night and the phone call.

It was at that point that the president's buzzer went off with the angry snarl of a rattler giving warning.

And it kept on buzzing.

I looked at Mrs. Scott. Was he furious already? Mrs. Scott glanced at her call director. The president was on the phone. What a day!

"He probably wants me, not you, Ms. Meredith." I wondered how far the efficient and insightful Mrs. Scott would have gotten in a world where women had an equal chance. Mrs. Scott was in her late fifties, and when she was starting out, she didn't have legislation to smooth the way. I remembered Daniel's view that most colleges would be better served if the administrators returned to teaching and allowed the secretaries to make policy.

Mrs. Scott came back through the door to the president's office, her face the color of newsprint. "Susan, would you come in?"

My heart started to pound. All right, he's said something to her. He's going to be *macho,* I thought as I went through the door Mrs. Scott was leaning against.

Because President Barker had a reputation for knock-down, drag-out arguments, I was steeling myself for that kind of a set-to, and it took me a few seconds to understand what I was seeing. Barker was at his desk, slumped over his blotter with his arms spread wide. A heart attack, I thought, and then I saw the red skullcap over his shock of gray hair. Blood! my thoughts signaled. I've had all sorts of Red Cross training, so I stepped to his desk to take a pulse even though I knew his heart wasn't beating. I took in the details mechanically. His eyes were open and his face was slack—total surprise. One of his arms had fallen on the buzzer and his phone was off the hook. Some sort of ebony sculpture lay on the blotter beside his head.

"I think I ought to call the city police," Mrs. Scott said decisively from the doorway. "And I don't think we ought to touch anything."

I lifted President Barker's hand off the buzzer and hung up the phone. "I agree," I told her, "but I don't think we have to listen to all that. I'll take that coffee now, and I think you ought to have some, too."

Mrs. Scott and I sat and sipped at cold coffee while uniformed men stood around and discussed the world series as they waited for the medical examiner to arrive.

When he came, it was a disappointment. He was a little man in a suit that looked as if it had been given to him for med school graduation and he'd worn it daily ever since. He walked into the president's office and came out thirty seconds later, scribbling in a spiral notebook.

"He's dead. Any fool could see he was done in by that piece of carving. Go ahead, take pictures," he said to the policeman with the Polaroid camera.

"Hold it," said a new voice with a ring like crystal in it.

I looked up to see a man who reminded me that I hadn't been romantically involved for over a year. Just standing in the middle of the room, he projected physical competence—a professional tennis player, a racing driver, or maybe a hit man for the Mafia. Then I saw his eyes, humorous and ready to smile even as he frowned, as if things were bad now but he'd make them better soon. I knew I was in trouble.

I get crushes. As a matter of fact, that's how I protect myself. I remind myself that they *are* crushes so I can keep my head straight. I took in the details of his appearance so I'd have something to build reveries on when it developed that he was married with seven children, or was a chauvinist, or somebody who voted for Miss Rheingold every year. A shade over six feet, dark hair and lots of it. His big nose kept him from being too handsome, but that probably didn't discourage feminine interest at all, just the opposite.

He seemed a textbook picture of the male without hangups, strong, alert, sympathetic. He wore a gold lieutenant's badge in a case hanging from his breast pocket. The identification tag said Bliss. Wow!

"I want all the harness personnel out of here. Now!" he said in a low but carrying voice. People began to leave fast. I didn't know what harness personnel were, but I reluctantly decided it included me, so I got to my feet. He probably lived on garlic, I told myself.

"Not you, ma'am," said the dream boat, giving me a peremptory head shake. "I want to talk to everyone who was in the office, starting with the secretary." He stared at me as if he were memorizing my description for a wanted poster. "Stainfield, get the preliminary statements while I look around the room."

He spun on his heel and went into the president's

office. A bald-headed man who looked as if his head had grown up through his hair put on a fatherly smile and walked over to Mrs. Scott and me. "Is there any more of that coffee? I'm Sergeant Stainfield. I haven't been up all night like the lieutenant, so I'm in a better mood."

Mrs. Scott was off for the supply room before I could move, so Sergeant Stainfield started interrogating me. He'd just finished his coffee when Lieutenant Bliss shouted "Photo" from the president's office and a man came in from the corridor wearing cameras and a bored expression. Then the sergeant started asking Mrs. Scott questions in a soft voice. When she got to the office, how had President Barker seemed? What appointments had been set up for the day? I thought that the investigation would go a lot better if Sergeant Stainfield were in charge instead of dreamy Bliss.

Mrs. Scott had recovered her composure and was able to tell a factual story. President Barker usually came to the office between eight and eight-fifteen every weekday morning. When Dr. Lawnover, his assistant, was in town, they talked over the appointments of the day for half an hour. Sergeant Stainfield broke in. "Is Dr. Lawnover out of town?" Mrs. Scott nodded, saying that he'd been addressing an alumni group in Sun City last night and wasn't expected in till the middle of the morning. Stainfield nodded and made a note as she went on. President Barker came in through his private entrance, and he buzzed when he wanted her for dictation. Usually, Dr. Lawnover arrived about eight-twenty and took in the pot of coffee she'd put on when she came to work. This morning, she'd asked the president if he wanted coffee and he'd said no. These were the only differences from any other day, except that he was dead, of course.

"Basket!" Lieutenant Bliss shouted through the

door. Two men came in pushing a wheeled stretcher and walked through the reception area as if they'd come to move a piano. Sergeant Stainfield smiled at my round eyes.

"We all have our ways of making a living. Now, Ms. Meredith, what was your business here this morning?"

Before I could answer, Lieutenant Bliss appeared in the doorway.

"Would the president's secretary came in, please." When Mrs. Scott got up, he gave me another look to make sure my appearance hadn't changed and then smiled at Mrs. Scott while he held the door open. Suddenly, he looked much younger, not a day over thirty. I decided for self-protection that he was a well preserved forty-five and had ten children.

"Why were you here?" Stainfield asked me again. I told him my story. He kept me going by giving encouraging uncle nods and twinkles, making only a couple of notes on his pad. He closed his book.

"Where'd you come from?" he asked.

Suddenly, I was dreading answering his questions.

"Well, I was in my office till eight-thirty, and then because I was nervous, I went for a walk on the quad. I got here about two minutes till nine."

He started to say something, but I thought I'd better tell *somebody* about the truck. The groundspeople who came running from all directions after the crash thought it was funny. A man named Clyde seemed to be receiving a lot of joshing for not setting the brakes. I didn't feel like walking all the way down the ramp to tell them the truck had almost run me over.

"Just before I got here, I was almost hit by a truck."

Stainfield looked puzzled, but on that topic, incurious.

"I meant where do you come from? I'm from Massachusetts, and I thought you had an eastern accent."

We discussed geography for a while, and then Lieutenant Bliss came to the door and beckoned Stainfield inside. I wondered if his first name was Lieutenant and whether he ever took up with witnesses. I wasn't showing much respect for ex-president Barker, but then, he hadn't shown much respect for me if I'd been hired because they thought I wouldn't try to make Affirmative Action work.

I'd gotten that far when the outer door swung open and Roger Motley appeared. If Barker had seemed bored at our interview, the vice-president for administration had not. He'd managed to turn the routine orientation interview into a series of sexual gambits that never quite crossed acceptable bounds but seemed ready to at any instant. He told me about his converted C-47 that was painted black, like Hugh Hefner's. It was called, he said, The Jolly Roger. By that time I'd started hearing rumors about him. He liked girls—any girls—any time. He thought of both the female faculty and staff as girls. After I'd been on the job for a couple of weeks, he'd phoned me, asking if I'd like to go "flying" and somehow flying seemed like something that ought to be banned in Port Said. I told him my boyfriend—nonexistent—would love to come. And that took care of that.

He was handsome, tall and strong-looking, with a classical profile, but his eyes frightened me. They were too close together and were the shallow gray of dirty dish water. Besides, he seemed so confident that women would find him pleasing that I decided he was downright repellent, something he hadn't picked up on. Now I noticed that his mouth was too small, giving his face a spoiled expression when he wasn't smiling, as if too many people had tried too hard to please him.

He winked, as if we had had an assignation interrupted.

"Hey, Sweetcheeks, Buzz is dead, they tell me. Who's running things?"

"Lieutenant Bliss," I said. "He's interviewing people in the president's office."

Motley gave me a smile that made my skin crawl. I'm not a Puritan, either. "I better take over," he said as he opened the door without knocking and vanished inside. The interior office was soundproofed, so all I heard was silence. After a minute, Lieutenant Bliss came out.

"Would you come in, please, Ms. Meredith?"

The president's office was quiet as a tomb. No sign of Motley or anyone else who'd been in there this morning. I decided Lieutenant Bliss was so used to having his own way that he hadn't even been disturbed by the Motley incident. He waited till I took a chair and then sat down on the president's desk. He gave me the smile that made him so young. "Did you tell Motley it was all right to break in here?"

"That was his idea," I assured him. He couldn't be *too* old. I wondered if his wife understood him.

"Mrs. Scott says you were together in the reception area when the buzzer went off and you both came in to find him dead."

I didn't answer immediately because I wondered why he was handling the piece of sculpture. He saw me watching and smiled again. I noticed his third bicuspid had a gold filling.

"The only fingerprints were yours on the phone. Everybody knows that these days. Too much television." He brandished the piece. "We also wiped the blood off after dusting this for prints. We use all the latest methods. We talk to everybody and put all our evidence data into a computer and then crank out answers. This isn't a locked room crime, so we're more interested in people who weren't on the scene than we are in you and Mrs. Scott."

I must have looked puzzled because he gave me another dazzler.

"Either Barker was murdered just before the buzzer sounded when you and Mrs. Scott came in to find him or he was murdered earlier and all the noise was just a red herring to give the killer an alibi. I'd say right now that because you and Mrs. Scott were together, the two of you are about seventy percent exonerated. Motley, I'd say, is only in the fortieth percentile, because he came in here and tried to take charge of the investigation."

Lieutenant Bliss was trying to set me at ease.

"Really," he said, smiling yet again, "what we do in a situation like this is talk to everybody. Now. Your appointment with President Barker. Did you expect trouble?"

He gave me that smile again and I decided it was an interview technique. Put you off guard and then the zinger!

"I thought we might have to state our views frankly."

He nodded. "A college education teaches you how to say anything and make it sound nice." He jerked his thumb over his shoulder at the desk where President Barker had been killed. "He was a little man, a male chauvinist, and a racist. Of course you expected trouble. Has there been any pressure on you in handling—" he glanced at his notebook—"this Naomi Wilson case?"

I stopped having romantic feelings. This was a murder case and this man was trying to solve it.

"Yes," I said. "There have been all kinds of unofficial pressure. What I wasn't sure about was whether President Barker was involved in it. I still don't know."

Bliss nodded. "What kind of pressure?"

I started talking before I completely organized my thoughts because I was trying to decide whether to tell him about the attack in the corridor on Saturday night.

I didn't want him to think I was some kind of hysteric. He probably had a lot of female witnesses like that.

"All sorts of delays kept coming up before the hearing. A number of people tried to dissuade me from pursuing matters, the most recent Saturday morning. Dr. Lawnover, the president's assistant, but it pretty clearly, but I didn't know if he was speaking for himself or President Barker."

"What about that attack on you Saturday night?" he asked. "Most women I know would have mentioned that first."

He looked at me, but he didn't seem disappointed. "Campus security reports all attacks like that routinely. Is there anything else that I ought to know?"

Thank goodness he had independent confirmation of the attack on me. Maybe he would listen. "This will sound crazy, but I think there's a possibility that someone tried to kill me this morning on my way over here."

I told him about the runaway truck and he looked grave. When I finished, he looked as if he wanted something more.

"Also, on Saturday night I had an anonymous phone call telling me to drop the case."

He put down his notebook.

"Tell me about the case. I've heard that colleges were the last bastions of male chauvinism, but what's in this Wilson case?"

"There are plenty of bastions here," I told him, "but the case itself is simple." He smiled at my feeble joke. We went over it and he agreed that it didn't look like much of a cause for violence. When I finished, he had another question.

"Why did this place have a compliance review and why did they hire an up-front woman like you? Why not some patsy?"

Bliss was really very good at his job, I decided. The questions kept coming and I never knew what he thought of my answers.

"A compliance review results from repeated complaints. When enough incidents are recorded, the review team comes on. Benson has a lot of federal money—student loans, equipment grants, project dollars. They were told to get an off-campus compliance officer or else the money would stop coming. I'm still surprised I didn't get more cooperation. If I were to resign and give that as a reason, they'd be in big trouble."

Bliss stared at me until I began to feel uncomfortable. Then I decided it was another of his interrogation techniques and tried to wait him out. Just when I was going to ask him a question, he smiled and smacked the piece of sculpture into his palm.

"This thing cost fifteen thousand bucks. Some artist back east calls it *Blunt Instrument*. He was black, named Biko or something like that. Barker didn't like blacks. There was a big hassle last spring where he had to claim he was misquoted. You might call it poetic justice he was killed with this. That would give it an ethnic slant. Would that make your job harder or easier?"

That was one really off the wall. Before I could tell him so, he opened his eyes so the whites showed all around his irises.

"Hell, it might even be a woman who did it."

Crush aside, I decided to call him to order.

"Lieutenant, that sounds like racist or sexist prejudice to me. Every campus in the world has a million motives for murder floating around. Why pick on ethnics or women?"

He resumed his normal tone. "A woman with good wrists could do it. If she could fight off a male attacker, she could do it easily. Get behind him and Pow!" He smiled again.

I was glad my crush on Bliss hadn't gone any further. Just then, the phone rang. He picked it up as if he'd been expecting it.

He said "right" a few times and "thanks" once. Then that smile came on again. "Your secretary doesn't like you much, does she? Stainfield almost had to break out the rubber hose to get her to give an account of your time this morning. I figure you didn't decide to kill Barker between eight-thirty and nine o'clock, especially with that truck trying to take you out in the middle of it. You don't like my ethnic theory, do you?"

He didn't wait for my answer but showed me three fingers. "Love, hate, money—those are the motives for murder. Who on this campus had those motives except the people he'd been dumping on, this Naomi Wilson, or some ethnic who decided to make him bite his lip for what he said last spring?"

I looked at the tip of my nose and blew out my breath, something I only do when severely angry and thinking hard. This Bliss would aggravate a saint. "Lieutenant," I began, not knowing where I would end, "given the many different people in the world, you have to posit other motives. College faculty live different lives from the rest of the world because they have different goals. I could name at least a dozen motives," I concluded lamely.

He smiled maddeningly. "The faculty? What about the students, the secretarial staff? Hell, maybe a groundskeeper did him in for walking on the lawn. Give me some of those other motives. Name three!"

I was about to tell him of the man who spent twenty years readying a review of a rival's book when the door burst open and a man six and a half feet tall broke in shouting and swinging his arms like a Viking berserker.

"Where is it!" he shouted rather than asked. "Where

is it!" he chanted, his long blond hair swinging on his shoulders as his fierce eyes swept the office. "The vandals have invaded the campus. Rats in the sacristy!"

Sergeant Stainfield came through the door after him. Even as he launched himself through the air, I noticed he was looking at Bliss apologetically. Although he was a good nine inches shorter and forty pounds lighter than the big man, Stainfield managed to bull him up against the wall and force his arms behind his back. The big man went Whoof! and continued his shouting even though Stainfield was mashing his face against the wall. Finally, the bald-headed sergeant took out a pair of handcuffs and punched the big man in the neck with them.

"That hurt!" the big man said in a loud but now normal tone. I looked at Bliss. He was holding the sculpture like a sceptre as he watched the two men tussle.

"Turn him loose, Stan. Barry, I'd be happy to help you if you'd tell me what you want so loud."

Totally without embarrassment, the big man stepped away from the wall and smiled at Stainfield as if they'd just shaken hands. He nodded to me and began to lecture.

"As I was saying, I want *Blunt Instrument*. Biko died in March. Since it has apparently been used in murdering that cultureless little freak, it is now beyond price."

He stopped to comb his hair with his fingers and looked arch.

"Not that Barker contributed anything. Anyone could have been murdered, but with that in its provenance, the sky's the limit. At one swing of that lovely object of virtue, the Benson Collection has moved to the forefront of academic collections west of the Mississippi. Therefore, I'll just take *Blunt Instrument* and put it into safe keeping. I always said it shouldn't be off museum property. *He* had no appreciation of sculpture."

Finally, I figured out who the berserker was; Dr. Barry Martin, the curator of the museum. I'd seen him on a talk show once where he identified himself as an aesthetician—a beauty operator. Bliss seemed to know him and even like him. Martin was reaching for the sculpture when Bliss moved it out of his reach and set it on the desk.

"Barry, whatever else this statue is, it's evidence."

"Sculpture, Harry, not statue. When can I have it?"

Bliss sighed. "OK, sculpture. Now. When you came storming in here like a roaring boy, you talked about rats in the sacristy. Could you give me a slower reading?"

Martin looked at me and bowed as if Bliss had said nothing.

"I know your father, Susan Meredith. I know his work, that is, the temple book, not the tax thing. He's an excellent man." Without pausing for breath, he went on to answer Bliss' question. "All this last week Alexis de Montremonte, that *faux francais,* has been visiting our collection. He says he's photoing up an article for Paris *Match* but since when do they do photo essays? I think that little excrement was getting ready to buy what Bronterre was getting ready to sell. Thank goodness that's been obviated by this oh-so-regrettable occurrence. Hah!"

He looked around the room. "Killed by a piece of art. It's poetic justice."

Both these men spoke of poetic justice. Weird. Bliss stood up to put his hand on Martin's shoulder and Martin sat down.

"Barry, tell me about de Montremonte," he said firmly. "Spare me the commentary on his moral character. What was happening?"

Martin sighed. "Philistines are everywhere. The trustees decided that since Benson had gone public, a little more flare would help the endowment fund."

He glanced at me. "Benson used to be a private institution with some class, but since we came under the state's funding, we keep getting presidents like that Barker poop. Well, Barker asked for and received permission to launch a capital appreciation program with the institutional investments. Those were the words. I think he saw himself as a fund manager. Anyway, he started plunging in the market."

He sighed as if his best friend had passed on. "You know what the market's been doing. He reduced the value of our holdings, Benson's holdings, by ten percent without half trying. Then he wanted to start in on our art collection to get what he called maneuvering room. We've had a knock-down and drag-out about it and I intended to take it to the trustees, but those cretins wouldn't mind at all dissolving the collection."

He stopped and looked radiant.

"That's no longer a problem, is it?"

Bliss surprised me. "Barry, old buddy," he said. "You've just demonstrated an excellent motive to kill your president."

Martin looked imperious. "He was not *my* president. Of course I had motives to kill the little potboy. So would any other curator, but they didn't and I didn't. *I* would strangle him slowly and then spray-paint him mauve for a Warhol centerpiece," he ended, smiling at the thought. Bliss spoke again.

"OK, Barry. I'm sure you don't have an alibi, either. But tell Stainfield where you were this morning. Ms. Meredith and I have to take the news to President Barker's wife."

Martin nodded like royalty and left us. After the door closed, Bliss picked up the intercom. "Stan, be sure to ask old Barry how he found out about the killing and how he knew *Blunt Instrument* was the weapon."

He turned back to me with that movie star smile.

"I really do need you to help me with Mrs. Barker. These things can get out of hand."

Three

One eye regarded us calmly, large as a moon, outlined in silvery eye shadow and long lashes. The other was small and bloodshot, a hole burnt in a drab blanket, but the voice was assured.

Over the couch behind her head was a picture that showed Eleanor Barker dancing in front of a Big Ten marching band. She wore a golden skin suit the color of her hair. In the photomural, she was cuddly, but thin as a whip. The woman who sat before us was imprisoned in fifty pounds of additional flesh through which the girl in the picture looked out at us hopelessly. That social smile flashed uncertainly for a second and then went out when she saw me looking at the picture behind her.

"You say Buzz is dead? I'm so sorry. That's really too bad, isn't it? Why don't we all have a drink? I've found it's a nonprescription drug that really helps me through those difficult times."

Without waiting for an answer, she got up from the couch, the smile flickering again, and crossed to the elaborate wet bar. Her legs were still good, and even carrying all that extra weight, she had the movements of a girl. She poured a dollop of vodka into an old-fashioned glass and took a sip before she added an ice cube. She hadn't looked for a response to her invitation. The question of a drink had keyed a conditioned reflex. When she was sitting on the couch again, I almost saw her addressing the Faculty Wives Club about a minor budget problem. Her tone was assured, though her words weren't.

"I really don't know what to do next, Susan. Neither of us has any relatives left. I suppose there are funeral arrangements to make or something."

She looked at Bliss, who sat beside me on the facing couch, his palms flat on his knees, watching this exhibition with a neutral look. Before either of us could answer, she started again.

"We shouldn't have let Roger talk us into coming here. We both had our pensions from the service, but Roger said Buzz had the doctorate and the team needed us." She stopped to stare at Bliss. "Buzz was so used to taking orders from Roger."

Bliss inspected his fingernails.

"Where were you stationed?" he asked casually. Eleanor began to babble.

"East of Sarawak. The boys used to call me the Queen Bee. I was the only white woman for five hundred miles. It was nice. I had servants, and I could put on a party for a visiting wig by just snapping my fingers. Everybody except Roger had a little indigenous friend. I used to think he had a tiny crush on me, but he was too chivalrous to say so." She smothered a burp. "Roger is a fine man. There was some kind of problem that Buzz never explained, and Roger took it all on his shoulders so the rest of us could retire at full pension, but he just resigned. Naturally, when he got the gang together again, we had to come along. It was so funny. Buzz was supposed to be in charge. But you must be starving. Here I am rattling away and forgetting my duties as a hostess. I think it's not gracious to have drinks without hors d'oeuvres. I have some smoked clams and things in the pantry. Buzz always wanted me ready when he brought home unexpected people. I'll only be a minute."

Bliss looked at me and shook his head after she left the room. I decided that Eleanor Barker was certifiably insane. Lack of affect in emotional situations, behavior structured by social convention, and a serious alcohol problem—they all added up. Crash of glassware came from the kitchen and Bliss was on his feet immediately, but Eleanor came through the swinging door with a tray of canapes still in their bottles and tins. She was crying and her tears were making tracks through that carefully made up eye, but she was smiling like a brave little girl who has skinned her knee. Not insane, her brains had been destroyed by alcohol. Then I stopped. Who knew what she'd been through or why she drank?

"I don't know what's gotten into me," she said as she put the tray down between us and began to open bottles and tins. "You'd think I'd know better, crying with makeup on. Well! You must try these little pickled corn cobs. Not a calorie in a dozen. Buzz used to say I was cornering the market in them in case of World War III. He used to be so funny, but he hasn't been funny since we got here. He had that doctorate and then he joined the agency right after Korea when he couldn't get a professorship, and I got taken on as a translator. I have this knack for languages. I went out there with French and Portuguese and now I know lots more. Then we all ended up in Purna and it was like fate. Everything was fine till Roger got in trouble."

She ran down like a windup toy and sat looking at us. I was about to say something when she started up again.

"I understand what Buzz's death must mean to you, Susan. The president of a college is like the captain of a ship, but you're like me. You'll just have to struggle along without him. You're sure you don't want a drink?"

Bliss took hold of the steering wheel and shook it as he looked sideways at me.

"There are guys I've put in jail who'd mourn me longer. She tucked him into the past tense like she would a paid bill. She didn't make one mistake and she was bombed out of her mind when we got there. Is she nuts, or are all housewives like that?"

Suddenly, I was furious at Bliss.

"Are you married, Lieutenant? Why don't you ask yourself what your wife does at home all day while you're solving crimes and judging people on insufficient evidence!"

He killed the engine and glared at me.

"I'm not married," he said. "Besides, what's that got to do with anything? My old lady had six of us kids. A little wine at Christmas was all she ever took. She loved my old man, too, and he was no prize!"

I was startled at his tone. He had sounded perfectly civil in everything he had said till now, but without warning, he sounded like a blue collar steelworker. I was surprised to feel my heart threshing in my chest like a newly caught trout. Bliss was irritating. He offered more contradictions than any man I'd ever met.

"If you're finished with me, Lieutenant, I'd appreciate being dropped off at the campus. I do have appointments."

He frowned.

"I can't do that. You're undergoing a field interrogation and it's time for lunch. Lots of women are housewives and don't drink. I'm not a chauvinist, you know."

I decided that Bliss was getting ready to put a move on me. Best behavior and all. I thought it might be mutually educational to let him.

"But a lot of women make that choice and suffer for it, whether they drink or not," I said. "I overresponded. Her behavior was shocking, almost worse than finding President Barker."

He looked young again. Even his lips looked strong. "I know a place with red-checkered table cloths and fine north Italian cooking, no tomatoes—guaranteed."

When I hesitated, he gave me that slow smile again.

The gnocchi parmigiana didn't feature tomato sauce, and Bliss, I discovered, was an interesting talker. I kept forgetting he was a policeman. He even conned me into trying dessert, zabaglione Inglese, and then chose espresso for himself.

"When I was on patrol, it was different, but now it's deskwork and interviews and I can't eat the way I used to. You mind if I talk about this case?"

I shook my head wordlessly. The Italians understand dessert. I'd have to run miles to work this off, though.

"Barker was killed from behind in his own office. His desk commanded a clear view of both doors. Whoever did it was someone he knew and trusted. That means it was a woman, an associate—probably a senior administrator—or an ethnic he didn't fear. That's why I had to get you cleared first."

I felt as if I'd looked over the edge of a great height. Me, a murder suspect? I put down my spoon and he went on.

"Eleanor Barker qualified on two counts. That corridor door was unlocked. Who ever did it came through that. Being an alcoholic sometimes can be an excellent alibi. She could have bashed him and gone home to start drinking. She didn't have a hangover when we saw her, she was working on a new load."

He stopped when he saw my face. "It's not natural to take the news of your husband's death that way, even if you didn't get along."

I'd been going to dismiss the idea of accusing Lawnover, but the attack on pathetic Eleanor Barker brought out my sisterly instincts.

"You seem to want double-checked alibis. How about Arnold Lawnover? He was in and out of the president's office all the time. He was an administrator. He can handle a club as well as Eleanor. Besides, have you checked his alibi? I think he might be the one who attacked me Saturday night. His job was in jeopardy if Barker and I came to an open disagreement about the Wilson case. He knew he'd be thrown to the wolves."

Bliss nodded agreement while he stared at his tiny espresso cup. I went on. "When the attack on me didn't work, he had to kill the president. What's wrong with that?"

"The same thing that's wrong with my theory about Mrs. Barker. No facts to back it up. I'll check Lawnover's alibis, for today as well as Saturday night. But I have something else on my mind."

I got ready to be difficult. He was about the most appetizing man I'd seen in a long time, but if he thought he was going to collect me like a souvenir match book, he was wrong.

He signaled for the bill and looked serious again.

"I need somebody on that campus who is trained to ask questions and won't be automatically suspected of working for the police. We don't have a backlog of information about Benson, and you can help us. You're new there and you're the Affirmative Action officer. I don't think you'd scare off the murderer. I can find out a lot off campus, but I don't want to put on a big show till we have things narrowed down. I'd like you to get into the gossip about the president and report to me at least once a day."

I didn't like the sound of this one bit, but he waved his hand when he saw my face clouding up.

"You're not being a police spy. It's gossip. When we find out who he related to and what people thought about him, we'll have what we need to know. After the fact, murder motives are about as obvious as red, yellow, and blue neon. In the meantime, I want to check out Eleanor Barker's story. If Roger Motley was his superior in federal service, it's odd that he's his second in command now."

He saw I still wasn't convinced.

"Think of it this way. You're protecting your minorities and ethnics. In the meantime, I'll try to pin it on a chauvinist. How's that, Susan?" he ended, slipping in the first name casually.

I finished the last spoonful of zabaglione. Bliss was as smooth as Italian dessert.

"All right, Harry, but how do I report in?"

Gloria Keeney gave me a sheaf of phone messages and said that Diane Sampson was waiting for me in my office.

"The important thing though," she began, drawing it out, "was Sergeant Stainfield came by. He really questioned me about you, not only whether you were here but about your relations with President Barker and whether or not you had a boyfriend. Finally, he asked if you were the hysterical type or a lesbian."

She stopped and looked arch as she examined a long polished array of fingernails that were like stilettos. "I had to tell him I didn't know."

"Thanks, Gloria, I appreciate the sisterly support," I told her and walked in to meet Diane Sampson. I always liked to see Diane. This time she was wearing a dynamite warm-up rig that I envied immediately. She got up from my chair and it was National Smile Week.

"All *right!* Come on in, Susan Mightywoman! You really got on that chester's case! Zat why old Barker's dead? He went nova when you gave him the magic lasso? That was a good move, getting those depositions from the other woman who left here before."

Her handsome face was a dark sun of loveliness. "You do a downtown job, Susie M. Downtown! I'm done with your chair. Sit some."

Diane was in physical education. She'd been an undergraduate star in women's basketball and volleyball and had trained with the men's track and field teams. Her master's was from the state university and she was now an assistant professor who had spent a brief period as the Affirmative Action officer. She'd made it clear she didn't envy me the job when I came and we'd become friends. She was in love with a professor of sociology I hadn't met yet, an urban specialist named Henderson. She scissored over to the visitor's chair and sat down as if it were a third grader's desk.

"OK. You got questions. How'm I feeling? Fine. This year Benson's going to the volleyball nationals. I tell the women. We gon stay. All the way. Title City. You know, coaching volley I'm meeting a better class of people. Now. What else you want? I got practice in forty-six minutes."

Not for the first time I wondered why Diane wasn't a fashion model or at least coaching at someplace more prestigious. Henderson, I decided, and then caught myself. She says she likes teaching and coaching here, so leave it alone. She hasn't told me about Henderson, so I shouldn't speculate. I took the bull by the horns.

"Diane. Why didn't you turn in the Naomi Wilson case last spring?"

Diane stopped smiling. "I did. Barker buried it. He de-jobbed me before I could quit when he saw what I was up to. He expected better luck from you. Anyhow there was no way these ofay trustees were going to overrule the man."

Diane hid behind street talk and her queen sized body

so her mind wouldn't frighten anyone. She was using it now. "When you put the same rock through their window, they probably gon do the same thing they woulda done with me. Lose you."

She stopped and smiled like the Shulamite. "Course, they's somebody else gon be the man now. Maybe he'll make a different recommendation. Since he won't have the gang with him."

That brought me up short. Eleanor Barker had mentioned the gang this morning. I'd assumed that since Barker was the new president, the rest of the administrators had been at Benson for a long time.

"What do you know about this gang?" I asked, realizing I was going to work for Lieutenant Bliss, just as he'd asked, and without giving it a second thought.

Diane settled back and put a long narrow foot on the corner of my desk and began to count off her fingers one at a time.

"One. Motley. Barker appointed him vice-president for administration his first day on campus. No AA, no search, no nothing. He the man's man. Two. Guy named Bronterre, one day later. He the vice-president for business and finance. Three. Cartwright. Director of external instruction. Four. Arnie Lawnover. He's the only local talent. He was nothing till Barker rode in. An assistant professor of educational administration who was going to be let go for boring students to death and not publishing anything. But Barker laid a hand on him and suddenly Captain Charisma was leaving tracks in the cement, walking heavy, you dig? Every other presidential assistant we've had here was a gofer—worked up the agenda for trustee meetings, kept the minutes, and showed up for the pres when he'd rather watch TV or something. But Lawnover's something else. He *interpreted* Barker, who was the little man who wasn't there most of the time. He got him out of that name-calling mess last spring. They deserved each other."

"Where did Barker come from and why did he choose somebody like Lawnover as a right-hand man?"

"Old Barker was no academic," Diane said, sitting up and looking serious. "He wasn't even very bright, but everything he did was smart. He took on Lawnover when everybody round here wanted him gone, so Lawnover knew Barker was the only security he had. He was glad to tell him the ground rules."

"How did Barker ever get named as president?" I asked.

Diane shrugged. "Why is the sky blue? The old boy network maybe. All I know is a guy on the board named Simmonds was the mover and shaker who eased Barker in. He's a bachelor and he puts up a lot of money for the discretionary fund every year, so that's how he gets a big say."

I had one more question. "Is there any chance that Lawnover will be named acting president?"

Diane let out a whoop as she got to her feet.

"No thoroughfare there. He makes enemies wherever he goes. The trustees can't stand him. Lessee! It's got to be one of two. Davers, the Provost, or Tate, the head of philosophy. Davers has the administrative experience; he was a gun in African AID, but Tate's the local boy. His grandfather was the first president of Benson when it was a private college. I'd say he's pretty high on the charts. I don't know which one you should root for."

Diane left with a soul handshake and I riffled through my sheaf of messages. What could all these people want with me? "Please calls" from Roger Motley and Dr. Harriet Guyon. "Like an appointment soonest" from Ralph Ruiz, editor of the student paper, and "Will Call Backs" from Mrs. Scott and Dean Davers. I was picking up the phone to see what Motley wanted when the door burst open and a storm blew into my office.

It wasn't Lieutenant Harry Bliss coming to sweep me off my feet. Arnold Lawnover, accompanied by two scuttling women who looked like sisters, stamped in, spitting tacks. He still wore a conflicting plaid outfit. He broke out in a spray of spittle.

"Misssss Meredith! I demand an explanation for your meretricious and unmerited remarks to Lieutenant Bliss. You're nothing but a troublemaker and a silly girl, unqualified, relying on your father's name!"

I'd taken a lot of guff from him before, but now I decided to call the meeting to order.

"Dr. Lawnover. This, in case you have forgotten, is my office. I do not intend to be ranted at in it. If you have something to say to me, do so in a normal tone or I'll call campus security and invite you to leave."

Daniel Derbyshire had a Guggenheim to spend in Britain once, and he'd found me a proper British nanny. Since then, whenever I found myself in trouble, I reverted to Mrs. Chambers as my role model in dealing with juvenile insurrections.

Lawnover stopped in mid-flight, a bubble of foam caught in the corner of his mouth. He began again more calmly. I didn't believe in his anger. He'd put it on to intimidate me. Then I noticed that while he was waving a piece of paper at me in his right hand, he kept his left in his coat pocket and my heart gave an extra beat. There is pattern in the universe, I said to myself while Lawnover went on in full flight.

"Do you deny you said I assaulted you in the stairwell Saturday night? Do you deny saying I had killed President Barker this morning?"

He inflated his chest so it stuck out almost as far as his stomach and threw his head to one side. It was a second before I recalled the gesture—Mussolini in a Lina Wertmuller film. I wondered if he'd seen the movie or worked it up himself. I've noticed that insignificant men tend to model their postures on dictators.

"When asked by the police," I began in my best Mrs. Chambers tones, "I suggested that you may have felt your job was in jeopardy after our talk on Saturday morning. No one else on campus had reason to assault me. I suggested it was strange you had a vague alibi for not being on campus this morning. Did Lieutenant Bliss say I'd said these things?"

Lawnover rotated his head like a robot and gave me the goldfish eyeballs again.

"He didn't have to. I deduced the matter myself."

Suddenly, Bliss filled the doorway.

"I thought this might happen, Lawnover. Now tell me why Ms. Meredith was the one you came to see?"

Lawnover lost his poise for a moment and shifted his gaze from one to the other of us. "Er—um," he said unhelpfully.

"Go on, Lawnover, parade your alibis," Bliss said.

Lawnover took heart and turned to the two pallid women. They really didn't look alike, but they gave the same impression of having been raised in a mushroom cellar on starchy diets. They kept their eyes on Lawnover with the obedience of multiple wives. Maybe he'd rescued them from the cellar. He jerked his head at the mousy woman on his left and lifted his lip in what must have been an encouraging smile. I felt nauseous. The woman licked chapped lips and I thought of the millions of men I didn't want anything to do with. I decided Lawnover wore socks to bed—the ones he'd worn all day.

She began in a tiny voice. "We had a good time Saturday night. Arnold was ahead of his work for a change, so we played Scrabble and I made popcorn and we went to bed early."

She blushed.

"I remember especially because Arnold had no mercy. He beat me terribly."

It became very quiet in the room, but the little voice went on.

"You see, he knows so many more words than I do," she said, the mouse looking up at her masterful mate. All the same, a tiny fire was lit in her eyes and I wondered about the double entendre.

Lawnover jerked his head again to signal end of wife's message. He waved the piece of paper in his right hand at me.

"This, Miss Meredith, is a speeding ticket. If you wish to examine it as the lieutenant did, note the time and place of infraction, Sunday night, eleven-thirty, Sun City." He continued to wave the citation like a flag, but I noticed he kept his left hand jammed in his coat pocket. "After that, we decided to stay the night there. We drove back this morning."

Standing behind Lawnover, Bliss shrugged and looked morose. I saw all kinds of loopholes in his story.

"I suppose Mrs. Lawnover was with you then, too? How far is it to Sun City?"

I saw that Bliss was inspecting the carpet as if pricing it. Lawnover smirked at me. I wanted to hit him.

"No. She had a meeting with her encounter group. My secretary, Mrs. Evans, accompanied me to the meeting. Eunice."

On cue the other pallid creature spoke her piece. She seemed a touch more together than Mrs. Lawnover, but not much.

"As the secretary to the executive assistant to the president, I'm *ex officio* corresponding secretary and treasurer for all Benson's alumni groups. I was there on business. Dr. Lawnover was kind enough to share his car with me. His speech was very well received," she said looking at him with an admiration that I found impossible to explain. "We spent the night in the Gateway motel—in separate rooms, of course. We decided we'd be up all night driving home at fifty-five miles an hour. We we came back early this morning. And then dear Dr. Barker had been murdered. Dr. Lawnover said that if only we'd come back last night, perhaps the president would not have been alone and would still be alive."

She actually brought a scrap of tissue to her eyes. I wondered why Mrs. Lawnover didn't object, but she was looking out the window as if she were thinking about making popcorn with a lot of butter on it. Lawnover's left hand was still jammed into his coat pocket.

"Lieutenant Bliss. The man who attacked me will remember it because I bit him. On the hand. Hard. Please ask Dr. Lawnover to show us his left hand, palm up, please."

Lawnover's mouth came open as if he'd been caught copping a feel. He jammed his hand deeper into the pocket as if it would take a subpoena to get it out. Bliss was suddenly very close to him. As Diane Sampson had said, nobody liked Lawnover—except those two women. I felt a lot better.

Lawnover glanced at Bliss and seemed to think things over. Then he took his hand out and extended it so everyone could see. It wasn't a pretty hand, hairless, the palm area small, the fingers thin and pulpy at the ends, the nails chewed to the quick. But there wasn't a bite mark on it.

I felt bad again.

Four

Lawnover and his retinue had departed half an hour ago, but I still felt cheated. Lieutenant Bliss—I really didn't want to call him Harry yet—had stayed on for a while, giving me examples of suspects who had every sign of guilt except being at the scene of the crime.

"That's why I didn't expect him to hassle you. While he was with me, I phoned the state police barracks and the Gateway Motel. His story checked out. Usually when people get off the hook they forget about the accusations. I don't like him either, so I checked further. He turned in the official car at ten to eleven and he had his secretary with him. The odometer reading matched a trip to Sun City and back. Finally, the chairman of the alumni group said Lawnover gave a dull but acceptable talk last night and the meeting ended late."

Bliss picked up on my pout. "You saw his hand," he said. "He's a jerk, but the world isn't as simple as we'd like it to be. Now, sound out everybody you meet about Barker and we'll tag up for lunch tomorrow, OK?"

I nodded, but what I was really wondering was how old he was. He was so calm and competent that he seemed middle-aged. He went off to the trustees meeting, and I went through my "Please calls." I didn't reach any of them, but between attempts, my own phone buzzed and Mrs. Scott came on.

"Susan, I want to tell you that the trustees have just appointed Dr. Tate the acting president. I think this Naomi Wilson matter has hung fire long enough. I made an appointment with Dr. Tate for you tomorrow morning at ten. The regular trustees meeting is next Thursday, so there's time to get it on the agenda. All right?"

It was very much all right. If the secretarial infrastructure had taken an interest in the case, Naomi Wilson would be back on the payroll sooner or later. I thanked her and made a date for lunch on Friday before I recalled that if anyone knew all about Barker it would be Mrs. Scott. Besides, she wanted to be friendly, and I didn't have too many female friends at Benson.

The phone rang again. It was Diane Sampson, speaking over the background noise of a volleyball practice —shouts, thumps, and the animal squeal of rubber soles on a gym floor.

"Sue-person! I knew there was something I forgot about that Lawnover chester. Last year, before Barker arrived when they were getting ready to tube him, he filed a sheet on himself as a protected minority. He claims he's ethnic on the basis of a Chinese grandmother. Personally, I'd believe a sex change operation first, but he's a shucker, not the rhyme for it."

I wondered why she phoned me right then. Before I could ask, she answered.

"The drum says his only alibi for this morning is his secretary. There is no number between them."

"How'd you know I'd be wondering about that, Diane?"

She chuckled like chocolate syrup being poured before she answered and hung up. "The drum knows everything, Sue-girl. If we find out more, we'll pass it on."

So, Lawnover was exonerated. Since Diane didn't like

him either, the data was firm. That explained why Mrs. Lawnover wasn't exercised over Lawnover the demon Scrabble player who beat her mercilessly spending the night in the same motel as his secretary. Susan, I told myself, you're coming on like the village shrew, and I rang Davers's office again.

I'd been dreading it. It's difficult to talk to an administrator who's just been passed over for the top appointment. Well, they get paid for that kind of trouble, I thought as I waited for his secretary to come on the line. Davers was out of the office but he wanted to see me. How about three-thirty? Fine. I had forty-five minutes, so I ran through the rest of the calls. Dr. Guyon was in class. Ralph Ruiz wanted an interview tomorrow afternoon. Motley was on another line and would get back to me. I balled up the message papers and made two points into my basket across the room. I decided to tag up with Naomi Wilson. She'd been a trooper about all the delays, and I wanted her to know how things stood. Her phone didn't answer. In ten minutes, I'd be seeing Davers. The administrative game consumes time for little result, I thought. Why wasn't I writing my book on computer applications to personnel work?

Davers had struck me as a decent sort on the several occasions we'd met, despite looking like the prototypical macho male. He was a blocky man with a large head that made you think he was bigger than he was. His office was decorated with African curios, souvenirs of his time in some international program south of the Sahara. At a party one time he'd been demonstrating with a broom how a particular tribe used assegais both as spears and swords. The surprising thing was his voice, low and quiet, just barely above a whisper. He'd been brought to Benson as a hotshot administrator, but the faculty grapevine told me that he hadn't been allowed to do much because Barker wanted everything channeled to the president. The faculty liked him, but I knew that an administrator who doesn't have any power is always popular with the faculty.

Today, he was standing with one shoulder against the wall behind his desk, looking out over the quad, but he turned around smiling when I was ushered in. If he was unhappy, he didn't show it. He winked.

"I know exactly what you're thinking. How do you address a guy who has not been appointed president? I'll tell you. Just the way you would if he had. Call me Marv, OK?"

I nodded and walked across to shake hands. That was refreshing, an administrator at Benson who didn't think he was royalty.

"I'm Marv, so you're Sue. I want to go over the Wilson case. Barker insisted that it went straight to him, but President Tate and I have talked and we agree that we want to institute some standard routines. That means I finally have something to do around here. Diane Sampson told me about the case last spring, but she resigned before anything came up."

He watched my careful lack of response.

"That's what the record says. I know Barker fired her. Now, I want you to forward the report to me. I intend to give it a positive endorsement."

I wondered what the catch was, but who cares how many teeth a gift horse has?

"Do you think Dr. Tate will accept the recommendation?" I asked, still keeping careful count of the teeth. Maybe he wanted Tate to look bad.

"I don't know what his views on Affirmative Action are, Sue, but he's a philosopher and he ought to recognize an idea whose time has come. I have a different motivation."

With an opening like that, I had to ask him what it was.

"I find something utterly repellent in a supervisor exploiting his secretarial staff for personal comfort. The compulsion is disgusting. If she caught his eye, he should have offered her a transfer and then made a move."

He stopped and looked out the window again. He had the shiftiest eyes of any man I'd ever met. Even when he was telling the absolute truth, the sum of two and two, say, you had your doubts. I remembered that Thomas Jefferson was the same way, but he was a misfit, too. I smiled encouragingly. There was something else he wanted to say. It came out in a rush.

"I was the one who requested the Title IX review. When they get a message like that from a senior administrator, they tend to move. Barker wanted to fire me when I told him, but Motley advised him in everything and Motley knew he couldn't get away with it."

I wondered if Davers had brought on the federal investigators to discredit Barker. Upper administration could get like an Italian city state—all motives were suspect. He gazed blandly at me.

"Maybe I thought Barker would be dumped, but my conscious motivation was four senior appointments without a suspicion of national search, evaluation of credentials, or anything. I have friends in the academy, and I don't want them thinking I'm a part of it."

He smiled lugubriously. "At least I think that was my motivation."

I was about to say something supportive when he broke out again, his face set and staring out the window. "So they go and appoint that twerp Tate who has a good head of hair and a granddaddy who founded this place, and nothing else!"

He dropped his head and looked at his lap. "Sorry about that. I guess I was really counting on the job. A few more years and I'll be too old for presidential consideration. I want you to know I'll do what I can for Ms. Wilson."

I picked up my unused notepad and prepared to go. Then I saw that Davers's face was congested with passion so that it was almost purple. He looked up and thrust his fist at me. Then he stuck out a finger and then another until he showed me four.

"One, Motley. Two. Bronterre. Three. Cartwright. Four. That afflatus cloud Lawnover. He consulted them daily about everything. As his official advisor and senior academic, I saw him once a week for fifteen minutes!"

He shifted his eyes from his fingers to me. "Sorry, Sue. There's nobody I can talk to here except you. Now I find out there were all sorts of things going on I didn't know about, and my name was being used. I'm supposed to be on that Education Continuation Project. The first I knew about it was this afternoon when I was talking to Tate."

Davers stared at me and then got up to stalk over to the window. "He wanted me to tell *him* about it. Hah!" He turned away from the window. "Tate's got the presidential presence already. Davers, your name is on it. Find out what's going on and give me a report and a recommendation. Last spring that project turned out one-fourth of the total credits Benson was budgeted for."

He was looking through me at the crossed African spears on his interior wall. "We're coming up for accreditation next year. If we're not squared around by then, that Title IX review will seem like a tea party. Susan, I want you to go over all lapsed and dismissed Affirmative Action cases in your files and give me a report. Everything since the review. First Barker and now Tate. Tate also told me my signature is on the endowment committee audit report. It's the first I heard of it, but he wants to keep his own name spotless, so I'm in trouble."

Davers sighed and looked at his hands.

"This all probably sounds self-serving, but if I let that stuff get hung on me, my career in education is over."

Suddenly, he was brisk and purposeful.

"So you see, my dear, I really need your help. I'll endorse the Wilson case. I want you to check out how Affirmative Action has been working here. I also would appreciate anything you can find out about the EC project. It will be easier for you than it will for me. All I can do is write memos. OK?"

When I got back to my office, I still hadn't made up my mind about Davers. He admitted that he was concerned to protect himself, and he made no secret of his desire for the presidency, but was that a sufficient motive for murder? Bliss would probably think it was. Then my phone rang again. This time it was Kenny, the track coach, wondering if I was game for a jog up the head wall. He didn't seem quite as interesting after I'd laid eyes on Bliss, but I did need my exercise after all this sitting, eating, and listening to other people tell me their troubles.

"As long as we don't talk about macrobiotic diets, fine. How about five-fifteen on the fieldhouse track?"

I was only starting to wonder if Bliss got any exercise other than punching suspects up—then I stopped. That was a stereotype. He didn't talk or act like a bully. I was pondering why I was spending so much time thinking about a policeman when my office door opened. I'd expected Gloria with some letters to sign so I didn't jump, but it was a woman of mature years, slightly overweight, wearing flat-heeled shoes and a flannel skirt under a mannish cut sportcoat. Hair, salt and pepper, short, parted on the side. She wore steel-rimmed glasses through which she inspected me in an annoyed-looking way.

"You're Susan Meredith!" she said accusingly. "I know your father. You favor him. I have a case. Aren't you going to ask me in?"

"Dr. Guyon!" I said. "Please come in." Harriet Guyon was already in. The terror of the history department, a distinguished scholar, an old-line feminist, and according to campus opinion, the most productive scholar at Benson. Before I could offer her a chair, she was barking words at me again.

"Diane Sampson says you're OK. OK, we'll see. I want to lodge a grievance against Benson University. Are you up to that?"

I wondered what had happened to common courtesy and decided it was a victim of sixty as well as the sixties. I decided to move with the world.

"They say you're a troublemaker, Dr. Guyon. Anything to that?"

Her plump face fell into a pudding and her open mouth made an O that matched her glasses. Then she laughed, a titter that became a guffaw.

"You'll do, girlie. You remind me of Daniel D. You take after him, I see. Well, here it is, short and hairy. Look," she said, pulling a stiff sheet of letterhead from her pocket.

The expensive paper had been crumpled and then smoothed out. The date was over a week old. I recognized the foundation—The Etchver Organization, the outfit that sponsored Daniel's temple book. It offered support to senior scholars in the humanities and social sciences for periods of a year or more. Although

Etchver wasn't too well known to the public, it was more impressive than a Guggenheim to those in the trade. Etchver gave only one or two grants a year, but the grant covered salary, travel, and project expenses, including secretarial costs.

I read the letter. After some boilerplate, it got down to cases. "At this time it is not possible to subvent the very interesting research you propose . . . This is in no way a negative judgment on your proposal, but rather . . ." and went off into inconsequentials that still said no.

Harried Guyon was studying my face when I looked up. "I don't think there's anything actionable on the surface," I told her. "Is there something else?"

Dr. Guyon nodded approvingly. "Good. You're not one of those knee-jerk injustice hunters. You bet your sweet bod there's something else. I was asked to apply, that's standard. All the preliminaries went like silk, but the day I got this letter, my case officer phoned to tell me I'd been turned down because the obligatory reference from the president of my institution was totally negative, calling into question the originality of my earlier work and the validity of my proposal. The letter verged on libel. My case officer was furious. He told me that the grant could still be retrieved if I made the institution back off by retracting the letter and writing another one."

Harriet Guyon's face was no longer a pudding. It was more a block of marble. A strand of hair had fallen over one eye and she looked primeval.

"That pompous little racketeer was paying me back for blowing the whistle on that Education Continuation project swindle. That shoddy little man who never had an idea in his life was calling *my* work into question. He hadn't read it and I doubt if he could have without moving his lips. But I fixed him good!" she shouted, shooting her eyes around my office looking for contradictions from the furniture. "I *ended* him!" she said in a harsh whisper, slamming her hand flat on the table.

I wondered what it was about the academic life that made people speak in italics and pound tables for emphasis. Then I took in what she had said.

"What did you do?" I asked, hoping I was not going to be confronted with a murder confession. Harriet Guyon's shoulders were impressive enough to get a lot of physical jobs done.

"I moved that the faculty senate of Benson University inquire into the nature, funding, and standards as well as the operations practices of the Educational Continuation project," she said, sitting back with the air of one who has done a good day's work. "But that's not enough," she said. "I want you to get into the dead letter files of that dead letter and find a copy of the recco he wrote." She smiled like a shark. "Then I'm going to sue this institution which has so grossly underpaid me all these years for the complete expense of what I lost by not getting the Etchver, plus punitive damages. I may retire on the proceeds. How's that?"

"That's bad," I said mechanically, "for you and for Benson." Damnit! The EC project was the only social outreach program Benson had. It was a good idea, training people up for realistic jobs that could take them out of poverty. Dr. Guyon's response to it was what she was quick to accuse other people of having, a knee jerk. If it wasn't on campus, it was on its face not worthy education. I probably couldn't pull her off her vendetta, but I could help her. "Do you want to sue or do you want the grant, Dr. Guyon? You know how litigation goes on a question of scholarly reputation. I think I can help."

For the first time, she looked doubtful, so I became decisive.

"I really think that would be better. You know lawyers! And after everything was out, they'd argue Barker was writing in his capacity as an individual so the university was faultless. That would be after they'd brought in that fellow who disagreed about your research on the origins of *Aucassin and Nicolette.* You know the state doesn't like to give up money."

I thought I'd gone too far. For a moment Dr. Guyon looked like a cannibal to whom long pig had been mentioned. Then she pursed her lips and stared at me.

"Call me Harriet, Susan. I'm perfectly able to take care of myself in an academic fracas, but I guess you're right. Have Tate write a letter of retraction and recommendation—and copy me in. Then, if the grant comes through, the university is off the hook. But!"

She scowled and her brows knit into a straight line so that she looked like Boadicea, Queen of the Ieeni.

"The investigation of the EC project goes on. That is a con operation peddling Benson's good name for money! Disgraceful!"

After Harriet left—we were now on a first-name basis in sisterhood—I sighed in relief. An enormously talented woman who happened to be married to Benson University. At one moment she was ready to bring down the whole institution because Benson's agents had done her wrong and the next, she was willing to put somebody in jail because they had smirched Benson's good name. I hoped that I never put my heart in the keeping of an institution. It did bad things to your common sense.

Whether there was a copy of Barker's letter in the files or not, Tate ought to be glad to rectify the situation. At least I hoped he would. Then I started assembling what I knew about Benson's new president. We nodded because our offices were on the same floor. He was tall, handsome in a presidential way, looking like a cross between a scholar and a Roman senator. He said little in administrative council, usually seconding motions or talking under his breath when something particularly stupid was said. I had no idea of his real capacities.

The phone rang again. It struck me I had a more intense relationship with my telephone than I did with anyone else on this campus. Tate was calling himself, not using Mrs. Scott. Like Davers, he seemed not to be hung up on his position. That was an advance over Barker.

"Susan Meredith, this is Charles Tate," he said smoothly, not tripping over a choice between Ms. or Miss. "Why, thank you. I guess it's an honor. Mrs. Scott was showing me the ropes and she has written in for tomorrow about the Wilson case. I'm seeing more people in a day than I'm used to meeting in a week and they all want immediate answers. Could you send me a copy of your recommendations this afternoon so I can digest them before the meeting? We philosophers like to think things over slowly. Thanks."

Since Tate had been a faculty representative of the committee that had unanimously endorsed my recommendation about Naomi, I wondered what he had to think over. I looked at the clock. Thank goodness it was five. It had been an incredible day.

Kenny was doing leg lifts when I arrived. He had a heavy build for a tennis player, but he was fast and strong, no two-handed backhands for him. Today he looked like a piece of lemon cake, blonde hair sun-bleached, his tan heated from within by exercise, and those perfect pectorals. He stopped frowning and showed me white, even teeth as I stepped onto the cross country track.

"I'd about given you up, lady. If you've had a bad

day, you better do some stretches before we start. If you let the adrenalin flow while sitting still, you're a sitting duck for a coronary."

"No more diet talk, Kenny, and, yes, I had a *baaad* day," I told him as I began to loosen up. He stood and scrubbed his face with his towel as he watched me.

"Come on, lady, get the old *gluteus maximus* into play or it will be *maximus* some day."

Kenny and I didn't have a romantic relationship, more like siblings, I guess. He walked around in circles while I did my bends.

"I had quite a day myself. You feel up to running the head slope—up? It's the only thing that calms me down. We have a bear of a personnel problem in our division," he told me while he took out a pair of hand exercisers and squeezed them in unison.

I was heated up now, what my grandmother would have called "glowing."

"Let's go. I didn't think coaches had personnel problems except who makes the varsity. What's happening?"

Kenny shucked his warm-up pants and set out after me at an easy lope. He ate up the twenty-five yard head start in no time and his breathing was as unlabored as if we were walking downhill in a cool breeze.

"I don't understand all the ins and outs, but one of the guys I owe a lot to is in a real jam. He got me this job after I washed out of World Tennis."

The track sloped upward for a quarter of a mile and even Kenny didn't say anything till we crested the slope. There was new sand on the track and it hadn't been packed down yet. My eyes were stinging with effort. Maybe I'd better jog more often than three times a week, I thought. Kenny started talking again as we came out on the level.

"I had a candy bar yesterday and I'm still ridding my

system of the poisons."

"Kenny!" I said, "No more of that. What's the problem?"

"Anyway, I asked if I could help and he said he thought he'd seen us jogging together."

I came to an abrupt stop.

"Don't stop," Kenny said, "you'll bind up. Walk if you want. I thought you said your wind was coming back to you."

I started running again. They couldn't have thrown Kenny at me!

"You're supposed to talk to me. About what? The Wilson case? What are you, some kind of a jerk, Kenny?"

He raised his sun-whitened brows in surprise. His eyes were like blue pebbles.

"It's no biggie, lady. Look, like I said, Coach Bell saved my bacon once. He wants a favor and he has an automatic yes. All he wants is for you to know all the circumambient facts. Hell, I don't even know what that means, but I told him I'd pass on whatever he told me. You want to walk or run?"

I was puffing from indignation more than the running. They thought this chunk of beefcake could buy me off!

"Let's run," I said, moving ahead where the track narrowed. Was any man as innocent as he seemed to be?

"Anyway, I said I'd tell you. Bell says Cartwright will resign if the case goes against him—and there goes the whole varsity program. He's come up with a whole bag of new money sources and we'll go right back down the tube if he leaves. As one jock to another, I thought you'd like to know that."

"No way, Jose," I told him, shifting into low gear, where the trail had gotten steeper. The trail ahead had been eaten away by early fall rains and a pioneer had veered off the sand and gravel up the hillside to avoid the slippery clay mess and started a new trail. I was just putting my foot on the rock that was a natural step when Kenny jostled me and I fell.

It was only a couple of feet, and I remembered to tuck, but then I was sliding on a clay bank that was as slippery as butter. "Hey!" Kenny said in a strangled voice. I felt something brushing the back of my hand and I grabbed for all I was worth. It was a shrub alongside the eroded path. It gave way, but by then I was beginning to think and I managed to grab another with my other hand.

Then I looked sideways and felt a pit open in my middle. I was hanging by an old Scotch Broom shrub at the head of a gulley that went down seventy feet at a stiff angle. If I slipped, I'd be all the way to the bottom. I looked up to see Kenny peering cautiously over the edge.

"You all right, Sue-lady?" he said.

"Get away, Kenny. I don't want you near me. I'm getting up by myself. Go on!" I shouted, really frightened. He was a trained athlete and not at all clumsy. I was huddled against the side of the cliff, but it didn't take all my strength. I wanted him away from me before I tried to start up. There'd be someone along pretty quick, the cross country team, for example. "Go away. You pushed me, you klutz. I don't want you paying off favors with me. Get!"

He got. I wasn't sure that it wasn't an accident, but nobody should be any stupider than necessary. If he was clumsy, he might accidentally push me over. If he'd done it on purpose, he'd try again. He shrugged.

"I can't stop here, I'll bind up. See you round, lady."

And he was gone, up and away where the track widened, his legs pumping like pistons, but I'd already forgotten about him. How did Cartwright, who was supposed to be running the EC project, get tied in with intercollegiate athletics? There went another crush. All I had left was Harry Bliss, I decided as I began to pick my bushes to get back on the trail. I'd never get this clay out of this rig. Shoot!

Five

I was being hustled by a master, and I didn't like it. Roger Motley was impeccable in a dark blue wool suit, but he was so relaxed that he might have been wearing a sweater and jeans. He had those heavy, unwinking eyelids that I always think are the mark of the successful womanizer, even though I privately thought he got off by giving grade school girls candy.

His name had appeared on my calendar without explanation, and we'd talked for thirty minutes without his offering a reason for the meeting. He asked me questions about myself and handed on tidbits about his own past that were supposed to make me curious. His own no-color eyes stared at me—or rather at my body, my hair, my mouth, but never my eyes, which is what people look at when they're interested in you as a person.

Abruptly, but for no reason I could see, his mood changed and he sat up to look at his watch.

"Ms. Meredith, this is an unwitnessed conversation. Drop the Wilson case. That's it. If you don't, things you won't like will happen. Naomi's not important, but you're bringing things to a boil and I don't like it. No more noise about it. If you don't make sounds, Tate sure won't. If you keep on, you'll lose your job and have a hard time getting another one. I don't care who your father is."

That made it clear enough. I refused to recognize that he was in a position to threaten me.

"Mr. Motley, I don't think you understand universities. There's nothing you can do to harm me. You're like an assistant football coach when the head coach is fired. You lost Dr. Barker, and nobody expects you to stay on here. It's not like the CIA."

He smiled as if I were the funniest person he'd met in years.

"Who said anything about the CIA? Suppose a rumor got out you were a doctrinaire lesbian? That's almost as good as being called a commie in the old days. You know how those rumors go on once they're started. Besides, I don't expect any trouble from Dr. Tate."

I saw no reason to respond to his threats.

"How did you come here anyway?" I asked. "Why aren't you heading up a mutual fund or sitting on top of a military hardware company?"

He seemed genuinely pleased at my questions. "That's the first intelligent response to me I've gotten on this campus. I've thought for a long time that higher education offered enormous opportunities for—oh, let's say—growth. When Buzz took this job, he called on me to help get the institution whipped into shape. I don't need the money. I have a fully funded federal pension. Besides, I have the Jolly Roger. If I wanted to, I could make a living flying charters. Who started rumors about me and the CIA? Some twerp on the faculty?"

I didn't intend to give him any idea of my source. "The faculty wonders why your man Bronterre is trying to sell off the art collection."

He yawned like a tiger while he stretched.

"That's old Barry Martin's concern, isn't it? We're not selling it off. That's for sure. Tell me, sweetcheeks, do you ever mess around?"

I've been around men a great deal, but there was content to his question that let me know I was blushing furiously.

"Mr. Motley, you can leave my office."

"I'm serious, sweethips. A girl like you. You're wasted in this place. You have great bones, a fine skin, and you look like you could really use your body."

His tongue crept out and took a furtive lick at his lips and I felt sick.

"If you don't leave, I will," I told him. He was on his feet instantly.

"Suppose I don't let you go?" he asked.

I wasn't going to threaten. I didn't know what I was going to do. Then I had an inspiration.

"Was that you attempting to rape me Saturday night, Mr. Motley? You strike me as someone into aberrant sex."

That cooled him off. His face which had been wearing a slimy smile, suddenly became as smooth as a sea-washed pebble.

I pursued the advantage.

"You've tried a number of things, anonymous phone calls, having that lout Kenny try to shoulder me off the track yesterday, but none of them will work."

The phone buzzed just then, and I picked it up before he could answer.

"Susan, this is Bliss."

"Promises, promises, Mr. Bliss," I said, thinking that if Motley thought I was connected with Bliss, he might back off. Motley sat down and pouched out his lips as if he were going to blow me a kiss.

"This is serious, Susan. I'm at General Hospital. Naomi Wilson's in the emergency ward. She's been beaten up and she wants to talk to you."

I said I'd be down immediately and turned to stare at Motley, who wore an amused look. I had the feeling he knew what the message had been. I made my face impassive and my voice hard.

"The Wilson case hasn't ended, Mr. Motley. Naomi's just been beaten up. If you'll excuse me, I'm going to see her."

He didn't seem surprised, but then he never did.

"Maybe her boyfriend and she got crosswise. You know," he ended not saying what I was supposed to know.

I left him standing in my office while I got my coat. When I left, he was chatting with Gloria. I wondered if he'd just been on the prowl for companionship. Then I wondered if he'd wanted to get my reaction to the news that Naomi had been beaten up.

I didn't know the quickest way to General Hospital, but I could see the spire, so I left the arterial and in my haste I turned the wrong way onto a one-way street. Then I saw an entrance that said emergency and took it. Inside, I saw that it was marked for Ambulance Only. By that time I had Naomi at death's door and I took the stairs up to the lobby on a dead run. Behind me, a black and white cruiser turned in with its lights flashing.

Bliss was talking to a handsome blonde nurse who wore patent leather white pumps to show off really sensational legs. He put his coffee down when he saw me and strode forward.

"What happened to Naomi?" I was asking when a voice behind me exploded in irritation.

"All right, lady! Let's see your driver's license."

Bliss looked over my shoulder and the smile left his face.

"Bliss, Lieutenant of Detectives, officer. What's happening?"

"This broad did a block down a one-way street and then used an entrance clearly marked Ambulance Only, Lieutenant."

"Citizen, not broad, officer. I called her down here."

I turned around and the officer blushed, but he handed me a pad to sign and gave me a copy.

"Sorry, ma'am, but I had it made out before I came in." He looked at Bliss, wincing.

Bliss had the expression of someone making mental notes.

"Come on, Susan," he said, taking my arm and leading me down a corridor laid with huge black and white squares of linoleum. I kept trying not to see what was going on in the open doors of the emergency rooms. Then I decided that what I was imagining was worse than the reality. I took a good look into one room and wished I hadn't. A smiling man in a blood-spattered white coat was bringing what looked like a chain saw to bear on a dirty cast leg. As the machine began to whirr, the child inside the cast began to shriek. I looked away.

"What happened to Naomi?" I asked. He was only taking off a leg cast.

"A couple of guys beat her up."

"That's terrible!"

"Oh, not so bad. Nothing important was broken, but she'll probably be taking aspirin to sleep for a while."

"You're callous, Lieutenant."

"No, Bliss, and I'm realistic. She won't talk to me, says she wants to see you. I think she blames me for it. I gave her a pretty hard time yesterday about her whereabouts when Barker was killed. Like everybody else, she didn't have an alibi. I thought it was only faculty people who didn't want to be tied to a time clock."

When Bliss wasn't around, I tended to idealize him, but when he opened his mouth, I stopped.

"Lieutenant, are you still thinking an ethnic killed Barker? Everybody I've talked to has a motive to kill him. Did you come on *macho* with her?"

Bliss flushed. "I questioned her at the station with a

policewoman present the whole time."

These men! I thought. "Why didn't you take her to an Italian restaurant the way you did me?"

This time his face grew redder and he tugged at his tie. "She's not my type."

"And I am?" I asked, putting the knife in.

I got as good as I gave. He answered immediately.

"You bet your sweet ass, you are."

After that, there wasn't much left to say.

We walked in silence up to a pair of swinging doors that Bliss elbowed open for me. Inside, Naomi Wilson was sitting on the edge of the bed, staring at a brick wall on the other side of an air shaft. She turned to watch us and I could see the extent of the damage. One lip was puffy, an eye was swollen shut, and she wore a finger stall on her left hand.

"Naomi! Who did this to you?"

She waved a hand weakly at me and glared at Bliss through her good eye.

"A black and white team put me up against the wall."

Bliss broke in, his voice grating like broken glass.

"You're accusing a police detail?"

"Nope. They know better than that in my neighborhood. This was an oreo couple. A big black dude I never saw before and a pale blonde guy." Both eyes closed as she tried a smile. "I was doing pretty well, but I lost my purse and that was it. They had me on the sidewalk before I could get my knucks out, but some friends came on and chased them off."

Naomi was quite a girl. She carried brass knuckles as a matter of course. I know I've been privileged all my life, but once in a while something like that happens to grind it in. Bliss looked at the two of us.

"Two attacks on women, and the women beat their attackers off till help arrives. *All right!*"

Naomi lifted her lip and then held her face.

"If you hadn't sent me home in that cruiser, this wouldn't have happened, most like."

Bliss gave the bed frame a shake. "If you'd told me anything, this wouldn't have happened. You keep not talking and a lot of bad things can happen."

I couldn't believe what I was hearing.

"I don't know what you're threatening, Lieutenant, but I know a first amendment lawyer who can be over here in fifteen minutes."

They both stared at me. Naomi started to laugh and then decided it hurt too much. "Hold it, Miss Meredith. I want the man to hear this. At first I thought they were a couple dudes driven to distraction by my bod, but it wasn't that. After they got in a couple of licks, one said, 'Tell that Meredith broad to drop your case or we're coming back with baseball bats.' Then they cut. I figure they were commercial muscle."

Bliss was immediately full of questions while I tried to think. I couldn't pursue this case if Naomi was in danger. When Bliss finally stopped, I began.

"Naomi, this has some connection with the university. I wonder if you know something about that Education Continuation project that you haven't told me. An Affirmative Action grievance shouldn't call for mafia tactics."

"That's what I've been trying to figure. I asked Diane Sampson to do some checking, but she says everything is on the up side."

Naomi had taken the beating, but I had to ask her.

"Do you want me to drop the case?"

For the first time, she looked unfriendly.

"Diane said you were a sister. You looking to back out? All I have to do is get lost while you bring this case to the trustees. I'll go stay with relatives out of town."

Bliss stepped between us, shaking no's. "That won't

do. If whoever is hiring muscle wants to, they can find where you'd go if it was anything from your past life. Then they'd have you outside this jurisdiction and you'd be noplace. Besides, you're not leaving this town till I know where you were between eight and nine yesterday morning. Tell me that and then we'll see."

Naomi peered out the window as if the brick wall gave answers. "Well," she said, opening her good eye very wide and staring at Bliss with it. "I was afraid it would be misunderstood, but I was on campus yesterday morning. I had some idea of seeing President Barker and asking him to give me my job back, but I lost my nerve. I was walking around in the parking lot when I saw Cartwright drive in. So I spent between eight and nine talking to him in his car in the lot."

She turned to me. I got the same wide-eye treatment. "I didn't tell you because I was afraid it would prejudice my case," she said hurriedly. "It's not what you think. Before he started trying to jump on my bones, he was a good joe. I said I'd drop the case if he'd get me back on the payroll, but he said it had gone too far for that, so we didn't get anywhere. I went downtown and checked in again with the Girl Friday agency. It's not steady, but it's groceries. I want my job back. I want my back pay. No other way."

Suddenly, I had a solution.

"Naomi, my father's been complaining about his secretarial help ever since I left home. He's between secretaries now and he has a manuscript to finish. I can phone him and set things up. He'd be willing to pay your airfare to New England and you could live in his house. I think you'd find him a more generous employer than Benson University."

She nodded her head decisively. Then she had one question.

"Live in his house? He got something on the agenda

besides shorthand and typing?"

I considered Daniel Derbyshire's record with women while Bliss watched me.

"I can phone him and have you on a plane out of here this afternoon. About the agenda, that would be up to you."

The one o'clock flight to New York wasn't full, and Naomi made it with half an hour to spare. Bliss insisted we have a sandwich in the Skyview Lounge.

"We do a lot of eating together," I told him.

He watched the United flight get airborne before he answered.

"What do you know about Cartwright? Does he seem like a guy who would hire enforcers?"

"I don't know anything about him. He takes orders from Motley, I think, and Motley would hire enforcers or do anything else he wanted. Have you done any checking on him?"

Bliss put down his beer.

"Motley, Bronterre, and Cartwright all came on campus within a week of Barker's arrival. You bet I'm checking on them, but it's taking a lot more time than it should. Do you know, not one of them except Barker had any experience in higher education? That explains Lawnover, he's their native guide."

I giggled at the picture of Lawnover explaining the native folkways of a campus to Barker's crew.

"Motley was with me when you phoned about Naomi. I had a feeling he wasn't surprised at the message. I teased him with what Eleanor told us about the East of Sarawak crew as if it was campus gossip, but he didn't seem troubled."

"Motley's a tough number," Bliss said. "Cartwright's the one who'd break if we could put enough pressure on him."

I decided there was something I had to tell Bliss.

"Naomi was lying about talking to Cartwright in the parking lot yesterday."

Bliss looked up from spreading horseradish mustard on his corned beef. He let the silence go on for a while before he spoke.

"She saw him yesterday, but it was between nine and ten. I've already talked to him. How did you know she was lying?"

There's no graceful way to eat a lavish corned beef sandwich, so I picked it up and said "Feminine intuition" and bit down so I wouldn't have to answer for a while.

Bliss said a four-letter word much worse than any I ever used.

"Don't give me that. I have more feminine intuition than any six women I ever met. How did you know?"

"I talked to him on the phone at his home at eight-thirty."

Bliss looked stern again. "Why does everybody lie to the police?"

"Because the police ask questions they know they'll get lying answers to? Why did you set her up that way?"

He sighed. "I know she didn't kill Barker. She weighs in at ninety-eight pounds. Whoever killed him was behind him and took a full baseball swing with that statue—sculpture. Forensics says whoever did it was between five and six feet tall. Even in high heels, she's not that big. But I can't let a suspect give me bird seed like 'I don't remember, Lieutenant.' The captain would have my badge."

It was his turn to take a huge bite of the excellent corned beef. I waited till tears from the German mustard came to his eyes before I asked my question. "Do you still think Affirmative Action is tied into

President Barker's murder?"

"You bet your—" He stopped in mid-sentence and swallowed. "You bet your sweet life, I do."

Then he smiled, a really *nice* smile.

"I can't fix that ticket for you because it's on the computer now, but I will write a note to the judge. Maybe he'll go easy on you."

At first Mrs. Scott pursed her lips when I asked to see a copy of the letter President Barker had written to the Etchver Foundation, but when I told her Dr. Tate would want to see it anyway, she smiled as if something were finally being done right.

Dr. Tate was standing with his back to the door, surveying a large oil portrait that now took up one wall of the office. It depicted a handsome man in full academic regalia who bore a striking resemblance to Tate. Tate explained the picture like a gallery guide.

"That's my maternal grandfather, Charles Tate Benson, the founder and first president of Benson. The Tates and the Bensons have intermarried cousins for a long time. Religion, the law, and education are family vocations. Every subsequent president saw fit to leave this portrait of Old Charley in the office except Barker. Now Charley's back and I'm here, too."

He gave me a smile too sincere to be spontaneous and indicated a chair in front of his desk. He sat down to display his well-kept hands on the blotter. I noticed that he had a nervous habit of galloping his fingers soundlessly on the blotter. Apparently he wasn't quite as at home in the office as he would have liked.

"But you don't want to hear about my family. You have a problem or you wouldn't be in to see the president—forgive me. *We* have a problem. Let's hear what you have to say and then I'll present my position."

Since he was holding himself defensively, I decided there was trouble ahead. I began with the Harriet Guyon affair. Tate was supposed to be a humanist and a scholar, so he might be in agreement about that.

"I'd like you to look at this letter Dr. Barker wrote about Dr. Guyon. She's understandably upset. The situation can be reversed if you write a more acceptable letter to the Etchver people. They're stuck with a clause in their charter requiring presidential endorsement of all candidates, even when the president's a fool."

A frown wrinkled Tate's forehead and he put on a pair of half glasses to read the letter. After a while, he made a chutting noise with his tongue against the roof of his mouth. He gave me that sincere smile again.

"I'll be more than happy to intervene in this situation. Dr. Guyon is our most distinguished scholar. Fine."

He sat back, a man who was hoping I didn't have anything else on my mind. I could see him starting his dismissal ritual, so I spoke up before he could get to his feet.

"There's the Wilson case," I said and he looked disappointed.

"So there is, so there is. Tell me—may I call you Susan? What is there about the case that isn't in your report?"

I could see that things were going to be bad. "Nothing, Dr. Tate. Naomi was discriminated against, by reason either of her sex or her ethnicity—it isn't clear whether it is one or both. She was terminated for refusing sexual favors to Mr. Cartwright. Under state and federal laws, she is entitled to redress. I have recommended past pay and a transfer in grade to a different office. As I said in my memo, that is small redress, even if Mr. Cartwright is disciplined."

Tate stared at me for some time before responding.

He acted as if I'd posed a classical problem in Aristolelian ethics. I counted to thirty while I waited for him to answer. When he did, I wished he'd waited longer.

"Susan, I hope you know I'm not a bigot. But philosophers—probably as a result of Freudian problems in childhood—like to have things clearly spelled out. *Was* it sex? Or was it *race?* That's the approach I think that would be fruitful. You admit yourself that you don't know."

Another one of those plain language analysts! Oh, Lord and Beulah Terence Turnbull!

"I think it was Longinus who said that motivation doesn't matter. Behavior does, Dr. Tate. I trust Mr. Cartwright wouldn't so have approached a white male."

That did it. The one thing your typical chauvinist can't take is any reference to homosexuality. I don't know why it gets to their poise, but it's a handy jiujitsu trick when they get too pompous. Tate harrumphed like Colonel Hoople and chose another destination.

"We philosophers like to contemplate the total surround so that we miss nothing, Susan. You're right," he said as if rewarding a bright pupil, "that issue is peripheral. But that brings me to another issue. Should we be invoking the august powers of the federal government in what is really a personal matter? After all, Cartwright's a man and this—Naomi Wilson—I've seen her—and she's what they call on the street, I believe—one foxy chick. Should we be involved in something so eternal, so primeval as male-female relations?"

I'd heard what he'd said, but I didn't want to admit that I was on the same payroll with such a jerk.

"I don't understand your point, Dr. Tate. You're saying that she has no case? She convinced me and a committee of faculty and staff that she was being exploited in a way other people in the office were not."

Tate sighed like a martyr.

"What I'm getting at, Susan, is that we have here in our otherwise *very* permissive age an old-fashioned situation. Mr. Cartwright, a man of normal appetites and a bachelor—I might add—sees an attractive female and—what's the phrase?—puts a move on her. Instead of responding with a yes or get lost, she mounts her high horse and in a moment of anger, gets fired."

"She didn't *get* fired. *He* fired her. And he refuses any accommodation."

"Please, Susan," Tate said with a gesture reminiscent of El Greco's Saint Sebastian. "Cartwright, whatever his faults, is a well-paid, senior, highly respected member of the administration of Benson. You propose to hold him up to public scorn so that little—" I'd grown to hate his pauses, so I broke in, "Chippy who's only making about nine thousand a year? Is there some kind of means test for morality?"

Tate didn't blush, but he looked as if his collar had gotten pretty tight. "I was going to say little lady who certainly doesn't look or dress like a cloistered virgin—can embarrass Benson University."

There didn't seem to be a whole lot to say after that, but I was hired to say difficult things.

"As a philosopher, Dr. Tate, perhaps you can correct me, but the central issue is not that Mr. Cartwright made a show of sexual interest in Naomi Wilson but that he made having sex with him a condition of her continuing employment. As of this moment, Naomi has not filed a brief with any off-campus agency, but she will upon my advice, if this matter isn't settled expeditiously and correctly."

Tate did what I expected. He got out of his chair and leaned his whole weight on his spread-out hands to stare down at me.

"Speaking philosophically, Susan—and I know that's something you young people seldom like to do—do you recall the circumstances of the passage of the federal act that established the program giving women job rights and you an occupation? How can you take seriously a law passed under those circumstances?"

I thought about Socrates taking poison because the laws had found him guilty and looked at this illegitimate Athenian. I didn't lose my temper and I didn't break my resolve about not swearing, but I decided it was no time to mince words.

"A good many laws have been passed under a variety of circumstances, but they *are* our laws. If you disapprove of them, you should, like Socrates, try to change them, not subvert them as you seem willing to do."

My heart was pounding in my ears and I knew I'd have a headache soon, but I now said what neither Tate nor I had wanted said.

"President Tate, as Benson's Affirmative Action officer, I am formally requesting you to enter the Wilson case on the agenda of the upcoming Board meeting. I will, of course, inform the appropriate supervisory federal agencies that I have done so. You may make such contradictory recommendations as you wish, but mine will not change."

Apparently Tate had thought he could talk me around, because as I turned to go, I saw that he had frozen into exactly the same pose as the man in the portrait. Both Charles Benson Tate and Charles Tate Benson stared at me. Neither of them looked happy, and Tate looked guilty. I wondered if he'd killed Barker and decided I'd ask Bliss if our new president had an alibi.

Six

Friday afternoon I gave my standard talk, "When Should A Woman Think Like A Man?" It was nothing revolutionary, some one-liners and a few zingers that added up to the truth that women are their own worst enemies. You wouldn't think a talk like that would turn on the middle-aged housewives who were the Women of Benson, but it did, and I ended to lots of applause. That always makes me feel guilty because all my standard talk says is that if you sit home and mend socks and let your life go down the drain, it's your own fault.

The question period was interesting because that's when I can look over the audience. I noticed Lawnover's wife and his secretary. I wondered if he let her out without an escort, and then I remembered he'd said she had an awareness group she attended. I decided that WOB was it. For a minute, I thought she was going to get up to ask a question, but a woman who looked otherwise sane asked me what to do if your husband didn't treat you like a person. I gave her the standard advice, get a job and get rid of the husband, in that order. That stirred things up because her next statement was that she didn't have any skills, as if everybody else had been born with them. She looked to be all of twenty-eight, so I replied rather vigorously and discovered that that, too, resulted in wild applause.

I was still pretty hyper when I got home, and I was

wondering what I would do when I walked in to hear the phone ringing. It was Eleanor Barker inviting me to "one last party" before she had to vacate the presidential mansion forever. The party would probably feature the East of Sarawak gang, but I didn't have too many occasions to wear my nifty Givenchy sport suit, so I said I'd be happy to drop by. I didn't feel too much like a hypocrite because I had a lot of pity for Eleanor—or the golden girl who was imprisoned inside her by time and flesh. When I parked half a block away, I hadn't decided whether I was soft-hearted or soft-headed. It came to the same thing. Motley and his crew would be trying to pressure me to drop the case, I was sure. But Eleanor struck me as a child lost in a crowd of mean adults with that bunch. Anyway, sisterhood often makes me do dumb things.

Going up the walk, it was like the first fraternity house party I'd ever attended. From the street I could hear the sound of at least two hi fi systems competing brassily. All the downstairs windows were lit up, and since it was a mild October night, they were open and the curtains were blowing in the breeze. The house would be jam-packed with people standing and sitting on the staircases. There'd be shrieks from the rec room in the basement and the sound of breaking glass from the kitchen. Despite myself, I felt caught up in a party mood. The front door was closed, but it swung open as I reached up to knock.

I was inside the door when I made two discoveries, neither of which I liked. Roger Motley had opened the door, and despite all the noise, I didn't see anyone else. Before I could sort out my responses, Motley was talking.

"Come on in, Susan, you're early. Eleanor's making Sarawak Sazeracs, a new taste sensation from the Far East."

I was almost ready to back out, but the door clicked shut behind me and Eleanor came around the corner of the drawing room. This time she was fully made up. She looked like an enormous doll, her eyes shining, sequins on her upper eyelids—and a complexion like a Kabuki dancer. Her breath smelled of fruit.

"Susan! I'm so glad you could come before the other guests! I do so want to have a talk with you. Roger! I've made up another batch of drinks, would you be a darling and bring us some?"

I could see why she'd be the Queen Bee. Despite Motley's considerable presence, he did her bidding. From the music room I heard male laughter. Apparently the East of Sarawak gang didn't count as guests. I followed Eleanor into her parlor and sat down where she patted a cushion for me.

"Susan, I don't know what got into me," she began as if speaking a piece she'd memorized. "There was no scandal about Roger and the rest of us. He's independently wealthy, you know, and because one of our team members who's no longer with us made a mistake, he shouldered the blame. He was glad enough to dissociate himself from a government that had lost the will to win in East Asia anyway. Besides, if he'd been at fault personally in any way, he wouldn't have qualified for a pension. Now. Is that all clear? Fine," she finished as if a painful task had ended. "Here are the drinks."

"Sarawak Sazeracs for mesdames," Motley said, mimicking a waiter. "Susan, you haven't had an experience like this unless you've had one of Eleanor's Sazeracs."

I'd been thinking about asking for vermouth over an ice cube, which is about all I ever drink, but a good deal of social pressure was being exerted. I took the glass and ventured a sip. It tasted both rich and bitter, and it was strong. Eleanor had put down half her glass in one swallow. Motley was watching me and smiling in that way I found so disagreeable, as if he were only waiting for a chance to find me helpless before he did something vile to me. Some women like that, but I never have.

My attitude must have been obvious to him because he smiled again and wandered off. Eleanor continued to babble while I twirled my stem glass and wondered how I could get rid of it. I was convinced that I'd been brought here for a purpose. Maybe it was to hear Eleanor's recantation about Motley. Maybe it was something else. Her glass was empty and she was staring at mine, barely touched.

"Susan, you don't like my special drink. You've barely touched it," she said, pouting like a child. Her eyes, though, held a pleading look.

"It's just that after spending time in Muslim countries, I've gotten out of the habit of drinking hard liquor. I wonder if I could have vermouth on the rocks?"

Immediately, she was all smiles.

"Of course, dear girl. Roger!" she called in a screech that broke her voice. He appeared like a genie on a chorus of guffaws from the music room.

"Some of the other guests have arrived, Susan, but it still looks pretty much like a stag party. Are you ready for another drink, Eleanor?"

He gave me that enigmatic smile again when Eleanor told him I wanted a vermouth cocktail. Then he vanished. Eleanor started again.

"I'm wondering, Susan, how that handsome lieutenant is doing, Mr. Bliss. He seemed so capable, but he hasn't found who killed poor Buzz yet. How have the faculty taken the news that Dr. Tate is the new president? Do they seem happy or not?"

Motley was back with our drinks and a dish of salted seeds of some sort. I took a drink of the vermouth and it tasted right. I wondered why I'd been so suspicious of any drink that Motley had prepared. I remembered one of Daniel's aphorisms, "Only a fool cannot conceal his wisdom." That was Motley's problem. He was dangerous and he didn't mind looking it. As a result, I was nervous whenever he was around. I remembered all the dirty tricks the CIA had been accused of for years and decided he was capable of them all. The seeds were good, though, salty and meaty tasting. I answered Eleanor's question.

"They know Dr. Tate. It isn't as if he were new and brought in a whole new senior staff."

Eleanor's head bobbed again. I'd said the right thing.

"I thought that was Buzz's problem, but Dr. Tate has decided to continue all the senior staff, although he had some question about poor dear Arnold Lawnover, but now is not a time for changes. Here's more people!" she cried leaping up to greet Dr. Tate and his wife. I stood too, but Eleanor swept them away, leaving me by the couch looking at a precise little man with straight dark hair parted in the exact middle over a pair of owlish-looking glasses. He barely came up to my shoulder.

"I'm Caswell Bronterre," he told me and I realized that he was the member of the East of Sarawak gang I hadn't met. "Hey! Eleanor's got some of these ghendo seeds! Try them, Ms. Meredith, they're great! I'd have some myself, but when I eat, I drink, and when I drink two drinks, I'd feel it. Three drinks and I'd be feeling you. Ho!" he shouted, peering at me through those owl glasses. "Ha!" he went on, "I'm going to have some anyway," he said taking a handful. "Keep an eye on me if I have another drink, though."

Seeing him shake them into his mouth like a small boy showing off with peanuts encouraged me to have more. I couldn't place the taste. If I hadn't known better, I'd have sworn they were bakery items. I asked Bronterre.

"Call me Cas. They use them in baked goods for flavor all over the Orient. Motley's been thinking of importing them as munchie novelties. They're the seed of the acara tree. Hey! I understand you want to compromise the Wilson case. How's this? If the trustees find for you—which I doubt—we put her on the payroll downtown at the Education Continuation Center. She gets her back pay and that's it. Keep her away from Cartwright. I never understood that. I thought he batted leftie."

What the little man said shocked me. He certainly didn't sound like Cartwright's supporter. My face must have shown my feelings.

"But the trustees have to find for her. The money scared Cartwright, but hell, he's small time. Besides, I'm the money man, and I know the real secret."

Bronterre had obviously been drinking.

"What is the real secret?" I asked like some kind of Mata Hari.

"It's not money. It's only numbers. Benson's got a lot of numbers. You interested in art?"

I gave the encouraging but noncommittal nod you give when somebody asks you that kind of general question at a party.

"Art, now. That's important. Money's just paper."

He was refreshingly open, quite different from the rest of Motley's group, so I laid Barry Martin's accusation on him.

"I understand our portfolio hasn't been doing too well lately," I said.

"Who told you that?" he asked. "We took a downturn at first when we dropped some of those dogs the finance committee had been holding for twenty years, but we made it all back."

He leaned close to me as if confiding a secret of state. "You can always make money in a down market. Hell, you can even make money in a sideways market. We had to sacrificc a little at first to get liquidity to move, but now we're sitting pretty. Twenty-five percent in T-bills and half the rest of the capitalization in street names. We have a strong position in petro shares and the rest in energy-relateds. When thc latc fall rally starts, we'll be ready to move and it will be good news tonight. Hah!" he said, finishing his drink and looking around. Motley came up with a tray.

"I took the liberty of bringing you another vermouth, Susan. I knew this old skin was going to want more to drink. You like those ghendo seeds, Susan?"

I started to say they were delicious when I discovered I'd have to be careful or I'd slur my words. Then, for no reason, I laughed. My lips felt tingly, my private sign that I'd had too much to drink. I'd had one sip of the sazerac and only half my vermouth, but had all the symptoms of being drunk. Or drugged, I realized. My mind seemed clear, except for the sudden mechanical impulse to laugh. Muscular coordination was a problem, too. I wondered if I could stand up. It was those ghendo seeds! Another CIA drug, I decided. Although I'd been munching on them continuously while he talked, Bronterre had been taking them one at a time. Now I saw him open his hand and drop them into the ashtray and turn on his heel to walk away. I'd been a fool, suspecting the drink when it was the snack! I still had a couple in my hand, and I carefully slipped them into my side pocket. When I did stand up, the room tilted. Instantly, Motley was at my side.

"Not feeling too well, Susan? Can you drive or would you like me to take you home?"

I didn't like either alternative. I was obviously in no condition to drive, but I didn't want to be any closer to Motley than I had been. I'd leave the party and sit in my car till I felt better.

"I want to drive myself—home," I managed to say.

Motley helped me out of the sofa. I was all right as long as I didn't move or try to speak, but when I moved, the universe shifted with each step. I might just as well be drunk. Motley tucked his hand under my armpit. I decided the only thing to do was to leave immediately.

"Apologies to Mrs. Barker," I managed to get out, thankful that I didn't have a wrap or a bag to manage. If I could get out the door, the outside air would help. I knew that these alkaloids were strong, but their effects tend to be brief. Motley was smiling down at me.

"I remember when I was young, Susan. It took me quite a while to discover my liquor capacity."

I knew it wasn't liquor, but there was no point in arguing about it. He took my arm, but instead of leading around the corner to the front door, he steered me into the music room where by now at least a dozen people were standing, talking, dancing. I saw Tate, surrounded by Eleanor, Bronterre, and Cartwright. And Kenny Sawyer. Cartwright had his hand on the back of Kenny's neck in a proprietary way and was massaging it as he listened to Bronterre develop some thought to Tate. Obviously, Motley's crew had taken Tate over as easily as they had run Barker. I had a second to see Davers and Harriet Guyon. By then Motley was talking in a carrying voice.

"We're going to leave you ribbon clerks here, Sue Meredith and I. We're going out on the town," Motley announced, and swept us around the corner and out into the hall after everyone had a chance to see me hanging on his arm.

He was enormously strong, keeping me on an even keel with his left hand as he opened doors and moved us down the front stairs. Some people were coming up the walk and he greeted them jovially.

"Come on in, folks, the party's just starting. This

little lady and I have business elsewhere."

That was all I needed. To be seen, apparently drunk, leaving the party with Motley. Then I knew what the situation was to be. I was cast as the young alcoholic whose judgment was not up to her responsibilities! The anger helped. When we got to the end of the walk, Motley pulled us up short.

"All right," he said, spinning me around as he grabbed both my wrists with one hand. "You thought I attacked you Saturday night. I could do anything with you if I wanted to, but I don't take what I can get by asking."

My coordination was affected by the ghendo seeds, but I managed to thrust my knee at him, but his outer thigh blocked it. I stamped down hard at his instep, but my heel slammed on the sidewalk. He lifted me up by my pinioned wrists until my face was only inches from his. When he bent his face to me, I tried to bite him, but he was too fast and I missed. His hand pressing against the small of my back thrust me against him as he buried his face in my neck.

I felt violated far beyond what was happening.

"Now do you believe that I didn't attack you Saturday night?"

He didn't wait for an answer because a car turned into the street and impaled us in its headlights for a split second. He put me down but kept hold of me as a horn hooted in the distance.

"My car is handy if you want to continue this," he said finally releasing and indicating a large dark sedan. "You can show me some more of your little girl tricks for fighting off rapists or you can relax and enjoy."

I decided that one kind of lesson Daniel hadn't provided was something in the martial arts.

"You don't want that," he said. "How about I escort you to your car? It's an MG, isn't it?"

There was nothing to say to him, so I pointed down the street where I had parked to avoid being blocked in. I hated having him keep a hand on me, but even though my motor control was coming back I couldn't walk the half block without help. When we got to the car, he took the keys out of my pocket and opened the driver's side door for me and put the keys in the ignition. Then he gave me his superior grin.

"It's a short-acting synthetic derived from the acara. But a number of people saw you leave the party in some disarray. I would drive very carefully if I were you. We don't want Benson's Affirmative Action officer to get arrested for drunk driving, do we?"

I managed to climb in and slam the door. He stood looking at me for an instant and then waved me a mocking salute and walked off, his silhouette vanishing after he passed the first street lamp. I had no intention of moving, so I took the keys out of the ignition, opened the window and lay back in the seat, breathing deeply. Motley expected me to react like a macho male, so he'd challenged me to drive home when I knew I shouldn't. I was feeling better by the moment. I could move and the world didn't jar off its axis. He'd know that. I looked at my watch. Although it was full dark, it was only eight. I'd wait half an hour and then get out of the car and use the standard drunk tests to see how I coordinated.

While I waited, I thought. I'd been invited to the party to be discredited. I couldn't imagine any other excuse for the widow of the dead president to invite the new president into a house he'd be occupying within a few days anyway. But I'd learned a few things, too. Apparently Motley was unhappy with my story of the gossip about his past, so he made sure that Eleanor set me straight. My talk with Bronterre had also been useful. While he was watching me eat those ghendo seeds, he'd talked about his work. Why was he so interested in keeping the endowment funds liquid? Daniel Derbyshire had invested in the stockmarket for years and I had learned something about seasonal cycles. There was no late fall rally cycle. It happened about Labor Day or it didn't.

I was going over what he had told me when a car stopped across the street and put a spotlight in my eyes. Two men got out. I was feeling apprehensive, remembering Naomi, but then I saw they were policemen.

"This is the woman, Thad. Radio in."

I got out and stood up, glad that the universe wasn't slipping away on me. A trooper in a white crash helmet and a leather jacket came up. He flashed his light in my face briefly and then put it away.

"Miss Susan Meredith?"

I was reaching for my driver's license, ready to point out that I had not been driving and that I could pass any inebriation test, when he spoke again.

"You're all over the airwaves tonight, Miss. Lieutenant Bliss has an all-points out on you and we received an anonymous call saying that you were driving a sports car in a dangerous condition of intoxication. They even gave us your license number."

I had a pretty good idea who had done that.

"Let's get the drunk charge settled first," I said. "I think it's some prankster, Officer. I'll take any test you want to give. I have not been driving. You can feel the hood of the car."

He nodded his head as if everything I said made sense. Then he did exactly what I'd told him.

"Close your eyes and touch your nose, please. Fine. Now, would you walk along the curb for about ten feet? Fine. May I smell your breath?"

I let him and suddenly remembered how long it had been since I'd been close to a man in any intimate circumstances. Tonight it happened routinely. *His* breath smelled of peppermint, so it was all right, but I hate gumchewers. Then he said "fine" again and walked over to my car. He felt the hood and suddenly put the flashlight on the roadway and got down on his hands and knees to peer at the undercarriage.

When he got up, he was both puzzled and unhappy. "You've lost some brake fluid. It looks like your brake lines are broken. I would advise you not to try to drive that car in its present condition."

Suddenly Eleanor's party came into focus. At best I'd be picked up for drunken driving, and if things went really badly, I'd be in a serious smash-up and the verdict would be DWI when I crashed into something. No wonder Motley hadn't been troubled when I didn't take his offered ride home. He knew exactly how I felt about him and he was counting on it!

Just then the radio in the squad car squawked again and I heard Bliss's voice saying he wanted to speak to me. The officer who'd inspected my car took my arm and led me over to the cruiser. The other policeman held out the microphone and turned up the volume.

"Susan, these two officers will be taking you down to the central station. When you get here, Sergeant Stainfield will pick you up. He's expecting you."

There were no doorhandles in the back seat of the cruiser, but other than a slight feeling of claustrophobia, the trip down wasn't bad. I wondered why Bliss had spread a net to find me. I'd almost decided I was not a suspect when we arrived. Stainfield was waiting for us on the front steps of the station. He didn't greet me as if I were a suspect.

"It's great you could make it, Susan. Thanks, Officer, I'll sign your card. Now, Sue, would you like some police coffee? We'll go into that drunk driving call later. We want you to do something for us."

All the while he was talking, he guided me along a corridor that looked clean but smelled dirty. After a moment I gave up trying to figure out what the various smells were. Stainfield was watching me out of the corner of his eye.

"This building is in use twenty-four hours a day, and they don't come on with the disinfectant till after midnight. I'll associate pine oil with jails for the rest of my life. Right in here," he said, opening a door that said "Interrogation."

I'd expected a room out of an old movie, a blinding light over a chair with the rest in darkness, but it was full of light with captain's chairs pulled around a table. The walls were painted kitchen-green, a color I've never liked. Stainfield went over to a hot plate with a frazzled cord and brought back two polyfoam cups filled with a murky liquid.

"You take yours black, I remember. Now, in a few minutes, I'm going to take you into a room where we have a one-way mirror set up. We have the two men who assaulted Naomi Wilson. They're small-timers, and what we want to know is who hired them. The lieutenant is softening them up. When he's ready, I'll go into my act. Then we bring you in to confront them."

As a paid-up member of the ACLU, I decided I objected to this. "I'm not a witness to that beating. I can't identify them!"

Everybody was trying to make me do things I didn't want to tonight. Stainfield looked at his watch.

"The lieutenant will explain everything to you. Let's go in. You'll see what Harry has in mind in a minute."

Stainfield hit the wall switch before he opened the door I'd thought was a closet and ushered me in to a dark room with a window wall.

"This booth is soundproofed and we're picking them up on microphones. Everything that is said in there is taped, OK?"

The room we were looking at was identical with the one we'd just left, but the whole ceiling was ablaze with light. Bliss was leaning against the table looking at two men. One of them, a black, was sitting in a chair with his big hands clasped between his knees and his head down as if he were going to sit that way forever. The other, an enormous fellow who obviously lifted weights, had dirty blonde hair and a small face that hadn't grown to fit his body. He was pacing back and forth angrily while Bliss watched him patiently. As I sat down in the viewing room, the blond giant turned on Bliss and pointed at us.

"You think we're dumb or something? You think we don't know what's behind that mirror? You got some stoolie stashed there and then you'll put us in a lineup and have them identify us. You finks! Well, we got alibis!"

When he spoke, Bliss's voice was quiet.

"Sit down, Lester. Sure you have alibis. You have a bartender-owner who says you spent today in his bar. He'll stick to that story till I tell him he's going to lose his license because all sorts of people with long records are congregating there. Then you and Tatum are going to be hanging in the breeze."

Lester sat down when Bliss told him to. Bliss looked at Tatum, who continued to stare at the floor. "How about it, Tatum? I just want to have some information. Who hired you? Tell me that and you can walk. Don't tell me and you're in plenty of trouble."

The black man lifted his face and stared in our direction for several seconds before he began to talk. Although his voice was almost as quiet as Bliss's, the menace was double that of Lester's threats.

"Tell you, Lieutenant," he said slowly, "anybody who talks to the police is in plenty trouble already. That means me or Lester or anybody. You can't protect them or us forever. Suppose you talk somebody into identifying us as stomping on that chippy—though we didn't," he said, interrupting himself to hold up a large pink palm. "But suppose. Whoever that is has to go back to the district. Sooner or later, some friend might think about Les and Tatum doing hard time because somebody talked. Only thing to do is shut up."

He stared hard at the mirror. "That goes for me, for Lester, whoever."

When Stainfield touched my arm, I jumped.

"Now it's my turn. The lieutenant will tell you what he wants."

It was like watching a television show. In the room, Bliss shrugged his shoulders elaborately.

"I was trying to meet you halfway, Tatum. I'm going to have to let you talk to Stainfield. He doesn't like you to start with, but that's the trouble with old-line cops. No principles, but they do get results."

Stainfield burst into the room with a shout that startled even me.

"All right," he yelled, adding an epithet that I had heard only once before in my life. "The alibi broke. He said he was just blowing smoke when he found out it was gross bodily damage, conspiracy and attempted rape. Leave these—" and then he said that word again —twice in ten seconds—"to me, Lieutenant. I got a little argument here," he said, pulling open a drawer in the table and taking out something I'd heard of but never seen, a black jack. He slipped his hand into a loop and slammed it down on the table. It made a loud, heavy thock that scared me and I was in a different room. I wanted to protest, but neither Tatum nor Lester took any notice. Bliss smiled.

"Stan! You never learn. We can't book these guys all marked up. They'd be laying Miranda and Escobedo on us."

Stainfield scowled.

"You college guys! I got a towel I put around this, and I guarantee, no marks. The elbows, knees, ankles, maybe even the crotch a little. They'll hurt for quite a while, but not mark one. Tell you what. Let's cuff them to the chairs and you go for coffee. Then we'll see."

I began to feel a little better when Bliss shook his head decidedly.

"No way, Stainfield. We got a good pinch on these guys, and I'm willing to throw them back if they cooperate—the broad wants to leave town—so I don't want them touched. I'm going for the witness. When I come back, the deal's off. This is the last chance going down, Tatum. No more stops after this."

Tatum unpeeled his lips from his teeth and then resumed staring at the floor. Lester had caught his lower lips between his teeth and was chewing on it.

"Lieutenant," Stainfield said in a wheedling voice, "you shouldn't leave me with them unless they're cuffed."

Bliss stopped to consider. "You're right," he said.

Lester blanched and Tatum shook his head as Stainfield opened another drawer and took out four pairs of plastic handcuffs. Bliss stood with his hand on the doorknob while Stainfield cuffed the two men. Lester's face was greasy with sweat.

"No violence, Stan. I'll be back in five minutes or less," Bliss said.

Stainfield smiled in a way Lester didn't find reassuring, nor did I. "Sure thing, Lieutenant. I'd like a prune danish to go with my coffee."

Lester started to say something as the door closed,

but Bliss was gone. A second later Bliss was standing beside me, but I was watching horror-stricken at what was going on in the other room. Stainfield stared at the closed door and then said another word I'd heard but never used and opened the drawer again to take out a dirty gray towel. He began to wrap the blackjack.

Bliss held something up to my face.

"I want you to put this hat on."

"Stainfield is going to beat on those two men, Lieutenant! You can't let that happen!"

Stainfield was crooning to himself as he folded the towel in a complicated pattern. The bottom half of his face had fallen slack. Lester looked as horrified as I felt.

"Relax," Bliss said. "Stan is the mainstay of the Providence Heights Little Theater. Lester's about ready to break. Now, will you put this hat on?"

I don't like anything I don't understand. The hat was a floppy cloth sombrero with a flower design in terrible taste.

"I bought it in a drugstore this evening. OK? We have to get in there or Stainfield will really have to start pounding on them."

As Bliss pulled me out of the door, I saw that Stainfield had wrapped the jack to his satisfaction and now was moving Lester's head around to find just the right spot. Lester was trying to twist away. Tatum was staring at the floor.

Nothing had changed when Bliss broke open the door. He was holding me out of sight around the corner as he shouted into the room.

"Stainfield! I've got the witness right here and she's willing. You spoil my case and I'll have your badge. Drop it!"

Stainfield faked a swing at Lester and then slammed the jack down on the table. Lester flinched twice and stared at the door open-mouthed.

"Here she is, Lester. She's going to cook you good!" Bliss said, drawing me into the room.

Lester took one quick look and broke out as he jerked his head at Tatum.

"That's not the dame we stomped!"

Tatum said something I didn't catch. I decided it must be *really* vile. Stainfield tossed the jack in the air and started looking like everybody's pet uncle again. Bliss kept his eyes on me, but he was talking to the two thugs.

"Well, boys, you ready to talk?"

I had a lot of questions. After Lester had made his damaging admission, Stainfield escorted me into Bliss's office, saying they'd be back in half an hour, but the time stretched to forty-five minutes before Bliss came back to toss his notepad on his desk. When he saw me, he snapped his fingers as if he'd forgotten something.

"Stan was supposed to get transport for you. Well, I can drop you off." He stopped and put on a serious look. "Do you feel like something to eat? An omelette? Tagging those guys cost me supper."

I had my own agenda. "What's going to happen to those men?"

He shrugged. "They'll be on the first bus out of town or they're in real trouble. We can't hold them even though they couldn't tell us much. Lester met a guy in a bar who offered a hundred bucks to punch up his girl friend, nothing serious. Lester split the take with Tatum, who's the expert and they did the job. We turned them loose."

This seemed all wrong to me. "Why didn't you get a lot of pictures of Benson's faculty and see if Lester could identify the man?"

Bliss stuck out his lower lip at me. "You think I'm

new to this? The guy he met in the bar was black, a guy from around the neighborhood who was leaving town. We got an ident on him and he spends winters in the south. He's gone. Somebody was using him as a cover. It's a dead end. I'm in enough trouble with the captain as it is. Look, let's take you home. You're not used to policemen's hours."

I didn't want to give up, and I had some things to tell Bliss about the case. "I've decided I'm hungry. Besides, I have some bits and pieces that you might find useful."

Bliss smiled and took my arm. A lot of men had been close to me tonight, I thought, but somehow with Bliss it seemed different. In the first place, I imagined that I could feel heat radiating from him. When we sat beside each other in his car, a Jaguar sedan, and he reached across me to lock the door, I felt quite dizzy, as if the effect of Motley's drug had flashed on me again. I told myself I really wanted to unburden all the suspicions and ideas I had about Motley, but I didn't believe it for a minute. I wanted to know Lieutenant Harry Bliss a lot better! Well, I'd given him an opening. I'd let him invite me out for a late night meal. Maybe he wasn't interested in me.

As if he'd been reading my mind, he took his eyes off the road and smiled again.

"We don't have to eat anything, Susan. That was just an excuse to get you out of our usual cop and citizen routine. When I go off work, I don't have anybody waiting for me, so different nights I do different things. You interested?"

Wow!

"I'm always interested in how people spend their time," I said. "Who do you find to spend time with in the middle of the night?"

"Most of the people I know, I met in the way of business, so a lot of them are night people, people with records. Sometimes I play chess with a blind con man I sent up for a stock swindle. He got crosswise in prison and had acid thrown in his face. Sometimes I work out in a gym run by a pair of brothers who used to be enforcers, like Tatum and Lester, only tougher. Other times I go home and read. Friday nights, I sit in with a jazz club at an off-hours joint trying to bring back the old days."

"You seem to have your life really organized, Lieutenant."

We came to a stop light and the red glow made him look as if he were blushing. "Harry, not Lieutenant. My life isn't organized, it's in a rut. I was married once, but it ended five years ago. When I was in uniform, she worried about what I was doing. When I made detective, she didn't know what I was doing or where I was doing it. Since my work involved prostitutes and drugs, she started playing dirty movies in her mind. It got to be too much trouble, so we ended it. She's married again out in a suburb. It all went to hell when she quit work and didn't have enough to do."

Bliss didn't know it, but he'd just passed a test.

"I haven't heard any good jazz for a long time," I said.

"I didn't say it was good," he told me. "Our trumpet man is better than you'd expect, but the rest of us are mostly enthusiastic. Sometimes a traveling professional sits in. Then it's something else. I can't guarantee tonight."

"Do you always guarantee a good time when you invite a woman out, Lieutenant?"

He frowned. "Nobody else has any trouble calling me Harry. What's your problem?"

"I'll have to see you play piano first, then maybe I can forget about the policeman. How's that?"

That was very much all right. I'd been expecting him to be a barrelhouse piano player, but as his group took over the platform, I saw he had classical training. The improvisations on the Ellington themes worked out by the clarinet, flute, piano, and vibes were complex and sharpened the appetite for more. When they finished, I decided this was a Friday night I'd like to repeat. I told him so when he came back with two more beers.

"There's a better market for law and order than there is for music. Besides, I'm a better detective than I am a pianist."

Suddenly he yawned. "Do you mind being taken home now?"

I thought of a number of rejoinders and discarded them all.

"Maybe you'll come up for a nightcap," I said. If he *really* was sleepy . . .

But his slow smile didn't disappoint me.

"You just want to know how a classical pianist became a detective," he said.

He told me more about himself as we drove through the empty streets. He explained why he'd dropped a serious interest in the piano for girls and football until we arrived at the University Towers. By now I was certain that there was a lot more to him than I had first thought. He took my arm and escorted me to the elevator. Before he could drop my arm and say that it had been pleasant and we must do it again sometime, I decided.

"Would you like to come up? I have a bottle of Courvoisier that I like to save for special occasions."

Then that smile came again!

We rode the elevator in silence. He was looking into my eyes and I was starting to feel a little giddy. When we stepped out into the hallway, I handed him my door key and he turned toward the door. His face changed.

"Stand still!" he said, squeezing my arm for emphasis.

Then I saw that my door was ajar, and the wood had been splintered. His arm flashed and I was behind him as he held a pistol and shouldered his way into the apartment. Once the door swung open, I glimpsed the chaos inside. My popcorn sofa had been slashed open. Then I took in the other havoc—the rug wadded up and flour dumped on it. I followed him through a rapid check of the apartment. Every room was the same—furniture slashed, jars and cans opened and dumped, bottles and boxes emptied. I sat down on a stool beside the breakfast bar.

"Why me? A random apartment on the eighth floor in a high rise?"

Harry put the pistol away and picked up the phone. Then he put it down and I saw that it had been pulled free of the wall.

"Not random, Susan, and it wasn't burglars. They tried to make it look like a search, but it was really an invasion of your personal space to intimidate you. You don't keep anything confidential here, do you?"

As he spoke I saw he was right.

"Nothing. Everything to do with my work is at the office."

I had a sudden idea.

"Was it Lester and Tatum?"

He shook his head. "They've been in custody or surveillance since early this afternoon. You said you stopped home before going to that party."

I didn't feel much like talking, and then it hit me. Strangers had forced their way into my home and destroyed my things! I thought about spending the night in an apartment with a broken door lock and no phone. Then I remembered what had been in train in the elevator up here. I was damned if I was going to let thugs spoil my evening.

"Harry," I said, "I'd rather not spend the night here with no phone and a broken door lock."

He had an odd look on his face for a moment, but everything came together when he spoke.

"I don't think we have a problem at all, Susan."

Seven

"Because I didn't want to look like the typical hysterical female, that's why," I told him. "When a woman who lives alone suddenly becomes the target of anonymous phone calls and unwitnessed attacks, there's just one explanation, isn't there?"

Bliss sighed.

"My dear, your shoe size is seven and a half triple A, but that's the only thing typical about you. And don't expect any Freudian psychology from me on that topic. Not after last night. Barker was killed and Naomi Wilson was beaten up. These are not your ordinary coincidences. Now you get around to telling me that Kenny Sawyer, accidentally or on purpose, pushed you off a running trail that could have broken a number of your vital parts. Then you cap that with the word that Motley tried to drug you last night. Why didn't you tell me then?"

I tried to think of a diplomatic explanation. "Things kept coming up," I told him and he smiled like a Turk.

"I'll believe anything you say. Haven't you figured that out? But I have to have some evidence. The cops who picked you up said you passed all the drunk tests that you insisted they give you. Nobody at the apartment house heard a sound from your place last night."

"What about my broken brake lines?" I asked.

"That was that phone call. Your brake reservoir was

empty, but the lines weren't broken. It could be anything."

"The ghendo seeds!" I shouted. "They're in my coat pocket. Can you do chemical analysis?"

He put on a long-suffering look. "Our forensics lab can take a toenail and figure out your height, weight, age and occupation. Of course they can."

I told him about the ghendo seeds, that they were the fruit of the acara tree, and then I decided he ought to be telling me some things, so I asked about his investigation of Motley and Barker.

"That's really something," he said. "They arrived in a group in this country about eleven months ago from overseas. All of them, including Eleanor Barker, are retired civil servants. Any more information about them is 'not in the public interest,' even for police inquiries on a capital case. How do you like them apples?"

"How did they get taken on by Benson University. I've heard of the old boy network, but these people aren't that."

He saluted me.

"We have General Walter C. Berry, USA, Retired. He doesn't know much about education, but he's the trustee who has the most money. He contributes to every major project on campus and there's more coming when he dies. I got that from Larry Simmonds, the clarinetist last night. He's on the board. The trustees were not too happy with Barker, but Motley and Bronterre seem to be first rate."

He stopped. "I tell you this so you won't think I spend all my time beating up on people with a rubber hose."

I gave a little yawn.

"No, I think you have other methods, but you haven't made much progress—with Dr. Barker's murder."

He gave me a smile that was both smug and foolish, I was glad to note. Then he got serious again. "Barker was part of the Motley-Bronterre-Cartwright crew, and I think he did was he was told. As long as he was president, they had no reason to kill him because a new officer's first act would be to replace them."

"Tate didn't," I said.

Bliss nodded in agreement. "Probably the long hand of General Berry, but they couldn't be sure. Besides, why would they want to dump him? I keep going back to that fracas last spring. Barker was a racist, and—"

I couldn't keep still after that. "This campus is like every other. It has enough motives for murder to start World War III, but academics go in for shaming rituals or nasty remarks. Look at Barry Martin. He thinks they were out to sell the art collection, but all he wanted was to insult them in front of the trustees. Harriet Guyon had a motive. Barker tried to poison her career, but all she had in mind was investigating the EC project. *That's* how academics fight."

Bliss looked bilious.

"How did a nice girl like you *et cetera?* I may not know much about academics, but I do my homework. I had the State Board conduct a spot audit of the project. The dollars check out, and there are bodies for all the student equivalencies. Harvey Welles is the trustee on the endowment committee, and he says Bronterre is aggressive, but a sound businessman. That leaves the academics and the administrators who aren't in Barker's group. Right now, I like Davers, but maybe that's because I don't have any other good suspects. It's right out of Macbeth. He wanted to be president, for one thing."

"That's ridiculous!" I announced, wondering why Bliss could start my adrenalin so easily. "Nobody kills anyone just to get a job."

He looked at me as if he wanted to take a bite. "How about keeping a job? Barker was going to fire him. It seems Davers requested the Title IX review. I don't know how Barker found out, but he did."

I suddenly thought of Gloria Keeney. I wondered if she'd been Davers's secretary when the letter was written. "He can't fire him for that! There are enormous penalties for retaliation."

Bliss shrugged. "There's always an excuse to dump an administrator. Anyway, Davers is all I have right now."

"What about Motley trying to drug me?"

Bliss stared out the window at the treetops of the park across the street from his apartment. He seemed to come to a decision.

"I'm going to break rules. First, I think there are two different things happening. Motley and his people may be crooks or creeps, but the killing of Barker doesn't fit that pattern. Look," he said, showing me his fingers. "Barker was killed by being hit over the head with a weapon that was handy to the scene. That sounds like a matter of emotion and an amateur. A professional would have made it look like suicide or an accident, or they wouldn't have done it in his office. Everything else that has happened is most professional. Naomi Wilson was part of that EC project and she was assaulted by people who knew what they were doing. Your apartment was vandalized the same way. Your car, too. Motley drugged you, but he has witnesses that you left the party having had too much to drink. The only slip he made was that anonymous phone call about drunk driving."

"The seeds," I began, but he shook his head.

"Even when we discover that they're a drug, who witnessed you eating them? Eleanor Barker and Bronterre. Are they going to bear you out or are they going to lie like rugs?"

I'd convinced this policeman I was on to something, but it didn't help! "What about the attack on me in Old Main? That wasn't Lester and Tatum. I could never have fought them off." Then I remembered that it wouldn't have been Motley, either.

Bliss's face became stone. "I know," he said in a strangled voice. It took me a few seconds to understand why he was upset, but when I did, my heart started pounding in my chest. This is love! I told myself, Paris and Helen, Heloise and Abelard, Romeo and Juliet, Armand and Camille, big stuff! I tried to take hold of my emotions, but this man was staring into my eyes while I was buck naked. Rimsky and Korsakov, I thought desperately, Walla and Walla, Ortega y Gasset! But it didn't work. He rose up on an elbow and put a hand under my head. His big chest obscured my view of the ceiling, but I didn't mind because his skin smelled like citron, though it tasted sweeter than honey.

I yawned and caught myself smiling. It had been quite a weekend, and the new week had started right. About an hour before the trustee meeting was scheduled to start, President Tate had phoned to tell me he had reconsidered his position on the Wilson case and would recommend reinstatement and back pay. Gloria hadn't been in the office, so I hadn't been able to share my good news with anyone. Even phoning Daniel's unlisted phone hadn't helped. He wasn't answering or he and Naomi were out. So I'd come along to the meeting, cheery and dreamy and for the first time since I'd been at Benson, I was content.

The wall clock in the trustee's meeting room said on the hour, but Tate hadn't shown up yet. Fleetingly, I wondered if he had changed his mind, but I decided that the Wilson case wasn't the biggest item on his agenda. Anyway, the meeting wouldn't start without him.

One of the trustees caught my eye and wiggled plump fingers in a greeting. It was the pink man, the clarinetist in Harry's jazz group. Now he wasn't wearing a pink shirt and matching bow tie. He was inside a somber suit, but his pink complexion still looked as if he should be attended by a physician. Then I had it. Larry Simmonds, the banker. I smiled back and he settled down.

Harry certainly had a variety of friends. He knew someone in my furniture rental company and apparently they had insurance against vandalism. They'd be glad to refurnish my apartment Saturday noon. He also knew a lock service that wasn't in the yellow pages and a home care outfit. When I got home Sunday evening when Harry went back on duty, I saw that the apartment looked as if nothing had happened to it. I went to bed and the alarm woke me twelve hours later.

I sat up straight with a start. I'd been smiling foolishly again. Mrs. Scott had just come in. She looked grim as she hurried to Larry Simmonds and began to whisper.

His pink face turned pale.

He got to his feet and began to clear his throat as if the words he had to say were stuck in his throat.

"There's no easy way to say this. President Tate is dead."

The low buzz of conversation ended and a laugh was cut short.

"He apparently suffered a heart attack on his way to this meeting. That's all I know, but it's certain that he is dead."

Simmonds was the picture of the student who is unprepared when called on. Mrs. Scott whispered something in his ear and he began to nod his thanks.

"In the light of this tragedy, I think we must amend the agenda to take up the presidential succession."

There was a sudden murmur of assent around the table and I had a flash that the naming of Tate as president had not been a unanimous decision. I wished I knew more about the politics of Benson's faculty and board. But if I really knew all the ins and outs, I'd probably be useless in my job, because faculty and faculty brats do tend to be busybodies. I suddenly decided that I was not going to stay at Benson. I'd never feel at home in it. Maybe it was administration I didn't like. Careful! I told myself. A certain lieutenant of detectives may be influencing you.

Simmonds was speaking again.

"In the light of our personnel situation, I'd like to ask our Affirmative Action officer to remain while the board goes into a committee of the whole to discuss personnel matters."

A burly man said "So moved," and the congregated students, faculty, and administrators got up to go, leaving Mrs. Scott and me as the only women in the room. The last two administrators to leave were Lawnover and Motley, who seemed pretty unhappy that I was remaining. Good enough, I thought, but why isn't there a woman on the board?

As the doors closed, Simmonds took off his coat and stared at us.

"All right. We had quite a go round last time and some of us lost our tempers. We had three candidates, Tate, Davers, and Guyon. I cast the deciding vote for Tate. Rather than go through all the hassle again, I propose that we take Davers and Guyon as the candidates and skip the campaigning. We've all heard it, and nobody's mind is going to change. I've asked Ms. Meredith to stay as an outside witness to the balloting if HEW wants to cut up rough."

He stared around the room as if waiting to pounce on objections. I didn't like the idea of being a tame witness, but I was seeing how the establishment worked. Simmonds started talking again.

"All right. This is a ballot for the Acting Presidency of Benson University, a term of twelve months with option for renewal. Mrs. Scott will pass out the ballots."

Simmonds hadn't struck me as very decisive at the Jazz Club, but if music was his hobby, administration was his business, and after some guttural mumbling, the rest of the trustees fell into line. After a lot of staring into space, they wrote names on the ballots and passed them up to Mrs. Scott and started talking again. For a bunch of people who had just selected a president for a multi-million enterprise, they seemed pretty calm, discussing golf, the stock market, and Benson's football season. Then I remembered that the rest of the world doesn't take academic politics very seriously, and I began to unfold the ballots as Mrs. Scott did the tally.

It was six votes for Davers and five for Harriet Guyon, which was about four more than I'd expected her to get. When Mrs. Scott announced the results, Simmonds marked his ballot and handed it over.

"A majority of the votes cast are now for Dean Davers. I'll entertain a motion to make it unanimous," he said, peering around the table. After a pause that threatened to become embarrassing, someone "so moved" and then there was a second. After that, the voice vote was carried. Simmonds didn't ask for No votes. The trustees certainly took direction well, I thought, watching Simmonds confer with Mrs. Scott before getting to his feet again.

"The agenda is mostly personnel matters, so I propose that we get word to Dean Davers that he's our boy and then adjourn. Is that OK with the chairman of the finance and budget committee? Harvey?"

Welles, I remembered, was a friend of Harry's, a thin man with dark smudges under his eyes and gray teeth who looked chronically morose.

"We're in a super liquid position, but the way the bond market's jumping around, I'm willing to wait a lot longer before trying to peddle those construction bonds. No problem."

Simmonds was just raising his gavel to dismiss the group when I decided that if finances could be discussed at this meeting, so could Naomi's case. I was on my feet before I knew it.

"Mr. Chairman. I'd like to suggest that since the board is in possession of all the facts on the Wilson case, it could decide it right now. She's been off the payroll for four months through no fault of hers."

Simmonds immediately lost his poise. He worked his mouth all over the lower half of his face. I noticed that some of the other men around the table seemed to be smiling. Finally he got a grip on an expression and put on a professional smile. I had the feeling his good will was about used up.

"Ms. Meredith, as non-educators, we rely upon the administration of this university to offer us alternatives with which to make judgments. At this moment, Benson does not have an administrator to recommend for or against your very ably presented set of protocols. Given that situation, we ought to let Dr. Davers get his feet on the ground. At our regularly scheduled meeting, we'll dispose of the Wilson affair—pardon, I mean case—" he finished to merriment at the foot of the table.

Despite his clear signal that the discussion was ended, I kept on.

"President Tate told me earlier that he would accept my recommendations on the Wilson case and Dean

Davers concurs," I said, determined to push things as far as I could. "He agrees that this is not an office romance."

Simmonds's face froze and he no longer looked like a beardless Santa. He wasn't used to contradiction.

"Perhaps when Dr. Davers sits in the president's chair, he'll have a different perspective. Meeting adjourned! I'd like the executive committee to accompany me to see Dr. Davers."

I felt as if I'd been fencing with an Olympic champion. He'd been perfectly reasonable, but like Tate, he'd seen the difficulty between Cartwright and Naomi as male-female business and nothing else. How was Affirmative Action supposed to work if discrimination was always labeled as "personal?"

Well, Naomi's case was to be continued for yet another month. At least, she'd be having a good time with Daniel Derbyshire. Then it hit me! What if the trustees had bought my recommendations? Would it be safe for Naomi to come back? Not if someone was willing to hire hoodlums to beat her up to keep the case from coming to a conclusion.

I put my materials back in my briefcase and walked slowly back across campus. There was something very odd about all this. The trustees knew about the case, so it wasn't a matter of keeping information from them. Then I saw it. If the board found for Naomi, she'd be back on campus—and all the pressures had been in the direction of keeping her off campus. Even Bronterre's offer on Friday night had been to assure that she worked in central city. If the board found against her, she'd appeal to an off-campus agency and there would be a new investigation. So every effort had been made to have her or me drop the case. I blushed. Daniel Derbyshire would have seen the situation instantly, but his daughter was a little slower. A *lot* slower, I told myself.

I was going to redo the investigation and this time I was going to find out what it was that Motley and company were so determined to keep hidden.

For once, Gloria wasn't on the telephone when I came in. She was polishing her nails with a suede buffer. She put it down to greet me.

"So old Davers finally made prexy! I used to be his secretary, you know, but we didn't get along. Say! You've got a really dreamy policeman waiting in there for you. I told him he could use your phone."

I wondered how Gloria had gotten the news so quickly. She seemed to be wired up to gossip central on this campus. Harry was reading one of my file folders with his feet on my desk.

"What are you doing, Lieutenant," I asked coldly.

"Are we back to lieutenant again?" he asked, his face really troubled.

I shut the door before I walked over to slip a hand into his shirt front to pat his bare chest. "I'd just as soon that Gloria Keeney didn't know how friendly we are," I told him. He looked as if he had plans that didn't involve a discussion of the case, so I gave him a final pat and moved off. He looked undecided only for a moment. Then he had a question.

"Do you trust your secretary?"

"Not very much. I've just about decided that she was the one who leaked the committee report to Lawnover."

"Good," Harry said, "then she'll leak the news that I've been reading this report on the Wilson case. I've decided it's the core of this whole mess."

"What mess?" I asked.

"Barker's murder . . . and Tate's," he said, watching my face.

The view must have been rewarding because he

dropped the case folder and walked over to me.

"Tate didn't have a heart attack. He was found at the foot of a flight of stairs with his heart stopped. That was the first report. The medical examiner discovered a big bruise between his shoulder blades. One of his dorsal vertebrae had been crushed with enormous force. Stainfield and I went back to the scene and found the weapon, a window pole. Tate had been struck between the shoulders. He was dead before he hit the floor. It was obviously an amateur."

"Why say amateur? This person has been pretty effective, hasn't he?"

He gave me that smile again! "He or she. It's an amateur who kills somebody on an open staircase that is momentarily empty. That's a risk a professional would never take. The staircase led from the president's office to the main floor. If someone had come up, the killer would have had to go back into the president's office where he'd be spotted or go down past Tate's body and take a chance on being seen there. It doesn't matter, of course, because he wasn't seen, but no pro would ever find himself in that kind of a position."

I felt obscurely irritated at Harry, but I couldn't put my finger on why.

"Are you saying it's an amateur because you think it might be a woman?"

He whooped with laughter that wouldn't stop.

"I have this thing going with an Affirmative Action officer. That means I say 'he or she' a lot more than usual. Everything that's happened so far could have been done by a woman except the attack on you. Anyway, Naomi's out of the running because she's on the other coast."

Harry moved to the door and opened it suddenly to find Gloria standing beside it with a file folder in her hand.

"Oh!" she shouted, "You startled me, Lieutenant."

"Miss," he said, "could you get us a couple of cups of coffee?"

If looks were poison, there would have been no antidote for the glance that Gloria laid on me. I decided for both our sakes that she should put in for a transfer immediately. Harry took a torn piece of paper out of his pocket and handed it to me.

"You said Tate had changed his mind about the Wilson case, and here's the proof."

It was a neatly typed and annotated agenda for the meeting he hadn't arrived at that had been torn in half. Under the personnel actions, he had written a series of notes in a minute hand that he would have been speaking from. I saw that the Wilson matter note said "reinstate—the committee—the AA officer—my own recco—facts; justice." The rest of the page was scribbled with underscorings and linings out, some of them so heavy as to obscure entirely what had been recommended, and the sheet ended at a ragged edge.

"That means Naomi can come back," he said. "I think she knows something that she doesn't know she knows."

I was about to agree when the phone rang. Since Gloria was out of the office, my extension rang. It was Daniel. Immediately, I was apprehensive.

"Is something wrong with Naomi?" I asked while he was still making sure it was me.

"Nothing to query the venerable parent about, just Naomi? Well, all right. Naomi is the question. We were getting along fine until Friday night. Then she received a phone call that upset her considerably. She spent a miserable Saturday and Sunday. Apparently, she was trying to get in touch with you but you could not be reached. She did not want to discuss the trouble. Last night she came down to tell me she was leaving. She couldn't stay longer. I decided she knew what she wanted to do and didn't need any argument from me so I took her to the airport and sent her back to you. I thought you'd like to know, so I phoned as soon as I'd done my daily three pages."

Writers! Nothing interferes with the writing stint! Daniel went on about how he'd thought she just might work out as a secretary and that if she changed her mind, to send her back. He hung up, saying he'd save his fond thoughts for next week's letter.

"Naomi's not at my father's house. You may want to talk to her again. She's been gone from there since Sunday evening," I said. "I'll bet those people of Motley's threatened her. They knew who my father was and they made a guess that I'd sent her to him. I bet they have ways of getting unlisted numbers."

"Who is your father?" Bliss asked. By the time I'd explained who he was, Bliss was nodding moodily.

"Sure, they could figure that out. I wish you'd told me who he was, we could have fixed up another safe house."

He strode over to the door and opened it on Gloria who was standing there with a tray and two styrofoam cups of coffee.

"Don't want that to get cold, do we?" he said, taking the tray. I hadn't heard a thing, but goodness knows how long she'd been listening. He closed the door again and handed me a cup. It was stone cold.

"At least they don't know where she is now," I said, "but where's she going to be?"

"Trying to contact you," Harry said.

Just then my phone buzzed like an angry rattler. I wondered how Gloria managed to make inanimate objects reflect her feelings.

"Sue! This is Bob Mercer. We met at the Angry Pomeranian about a month ago and I've been out of town. Charlie Debner introduced us. I'm the guy with the walrus mustache and the gold vest."

"Hello, Bob," I said uncertainly, but he rushed right on. "I was going to ask you for a date some time but a woman came in where I work so I'll be seeing you in a different context for a while."

"Let's keep our contexts immaculate, Bob," I told him. He'd seemed pleasant enough. "What's the new context?"

"Community Legal Services is where I work. I'm a lawyer. She's suing you—oh, not you personally, but Benson University."

I felt as if I'd cornered in a sports car through the windmill corner at LeMans. "Could you give me some background for our lawyers? First off, why me?"

"She hears you're OK and she wants justice, not just process of law. She doesn't speak English all that well, but she's not dumb. She says she's been trying to get in touch with you for over a week but keeps getting shortstopped. That's why I phoned."

The damned Gloria!

"I want to talk to her, too. What's her name?" I asked, getting ready to write on my legal pad, knowing that he was reading facts off a similar pad in his office.

"Rosa Puertas. She wants to sue for false advertising and failure to perform a contract. Wait! It's not one of those monkeyshine cases. She's got a legitimate plea. She's been enrolled in that Education Continuation project for over two years. She says her training has been a farce. She tried to get taken on by a local company and they laughed at her."

I felt my face flush with anger. Some half-trained, bigoted personnel officer playing with his power over someone who didn't have a great deal of self-confidence to start with. Then I remembered all the static I'd been hearing about the EC project. I'd said I was going to reinvestigate the whole thing, and now I had the perfect reason. I wondered how much of this I should tell Harry.

When I hung up, I recalled that only fools and criminals don't pass relevant information on to the authorities. I told him all about Rosa Puertas and what I hoped to do.

"I've been slow on the uptake. Harriet Guyon has been saying there was something wrong with the project, but I thought it was the ranting of a traditional academic. Gloria Keeney has been shortstopping calls to me from a woman who claims that the training she received in the project was inadequate. If Tate was killed because he was going to call for the reinstatement of Naomi Wilson, there must be a connection with the project."

Harry didn't look convinced, but at least I'd told him what I knew or suspected.

"I'm not going to put out an all points on Naomi, but I will have the downstate police stake out her parents' home. Whoever was trying to shut her up figured she'd gone to your father's house. That means they'll be looking for her to go to her own home or yours. We'll have people waiting. In the meantime, why don't you see what you can find out from this Rosa Puertas."

"I'll do that," I said, "but first I want to see what I can shake out of Gloria Keeney."

After Harry left, I didn't call Gloria in immediately because I wanted to do some serious brooding before I did anything else. Naomi wasn't going downstate to her parents' home. We'd discussed that earlier and decided against it. If Naomi was anyplace in town, it would be at Diane Sampson's. They knew each other and they were friends. I almost reached for the phone when I remembered that Gloria was almost certainly involved. I don't like to manipulate a sister, but she had been doing everything in her power to keep me from being effective. Come *on*, Susan, I told myself, if you can't handle this, you don't belong here.

I opened my door to call Gloria in and saw that she was, as usual, on the phone, having what was obviously a private conversation, her voice low and her hand shielding her mouth.

"Yes, Ms. Meredith," she said in a louder voice to inform whoever she was talking to of what had happened.

"When you're finished, please come in and bring your book for some dictation," I said.

Gloria dismissed me cooly and I went back to sit down and be magisterial. When she came in, Gloria's face was flushed. She was ready for argument, steadfast in denying that she'd kept Rosa Puertas from speaking to me. But I wasn't ready to bring that up. I put on my most sisterly manner.

"How are things going for you in the EC project, Gloria? You're a senior now?"

She hadn't expected this question. She stared out the window a second or two. "Fine. I'll be graduating this spring. It's been a very interesting experience. And I'm grateful to be able to work and learn at the same time," she said, quoting the brochure.

I didn't like this cat and mousing, but she wasn't going to reveal anything voluntarily. "What areas of sociology are you specializing in?" I went on.

"Oh, just general sociology," she said, gathering confidence. "It's part of the program that we have generalists for faculty instead of the professional specialists who seem to be all that Benson has in the regular departments. We have a bunch of very young and enthusiastic instructors. Mr. Cartwright says that the general problems the world faces have to be solved by young generalists, not old fogies who are locked into specialties."

I could see at least four fallacies in that last speech, but even generalists have to know *something*. "Well, that's nice. I have a memo for you. I'd like you to work up a stencil for it and then let me proofread it before it's run off."

Dictation is something I don't do well, but I've kept working at it. Usually I tell my secretary what I'm attempting to do and give the background of the memo so that if something isn't clear, the secretary can catch it. I'd used this technique with Gloria and she'd wonder if I changed methods.

"This memo copies in the sociology department, but it's addressed to three senior faculty. C. Wright Mills, David Riesman, and Emile Durkheim."

I stopped, wondering if I'd gone too far, but Gloria looked up from her pad. "Is that S-E-A-W-R-I-G-H-T?"

Rosa Puertas had a case. If a senior in sociology in the project didn't recognize that three world famous sociologists were not in Benson's sociology department, the project was little more than a mail-order degree school. I told Gloria I'd changed my mind about the memo and asked her to make an appointment for me with Dean Davers for later in the afternoon.

Eight

Bob Mercer knew what he was talking about. Rosa Puertas indeed had a case. All her work in the EC project had been Mickey Mouse, sitting in a circle and exchanging anecdotes for several hours a week with post baccalaureate students for "teachers." Her transcripts showed courses with high-sounding titles that were also offered by qualified faculty at Benson, but there were no textbooks, just an endless offering of "testimonies" on a variety of topics. I told her that Benson would make appropriate recompense. Mercer agreed to hold off filing anything if I got back to him within the week. I left his office on the run. This must have been why Motley and Cartwright were so eager to keep Naomi off campus. She knew something about the low quality of instruction.

My appointment with Davers wasn't until late afternoon, so I stopped at the cafeteria for a salad and a glass of milk. I'd just sat down when a mousy little woman sat down beside me. She started telling me how much she'd enjoyed my talk last Friday afternoon. As she spoke, I realized she was either Arnold Lawnover's wife or his secretary. Wife, I finally decided.

"You seem so assured when you talk, Miss Meredith —I mean Susan. I'm—I'm Daphne," she said in a way that showed she hadn't had a personal identification for some time. "I—I found it very interesting. You really mean it when you say that every adult is a citizen and everyone has rights, even housewives."

Daphne Lawnover was at least five years older than I, but she made me feel antique. She was one of those unlucky women who never get beyond a conception of self that means being daddy's little girl. It figured Lawnover's wife would not have a very clear idea of her rights. I nodded encouragingly, and sure enough, she came on.

"You said that after the state ERA passed, I—um—a wife has a corporate interest in any property the couple have bought during the marriage. Does that include the house? Even if it isn't in her name?"

Since I'd been working with women who came to grief through marriage, it was a question I'd heard often. Clearly, Lawnover would not have married a woman who constituted any kind of threat. I wondered how he managed to get title without her name on the deed. Before I could ask, she spoke again.

"Well, they, they have the house in their name."

This was getting embarrassing. I didn't want to pry, but Daphne had a problem that had bothered her enough to air it to a stranger and I decided I had to help. "Are you married to him or merely living together?" I asked.

She turned bright red, gave me a quick nod and then turned ashen. I was about to ask whose name the house was in when she pushed her chair over backward and was up and running out of the cafeteria as if I'd offered to bite her. I wondered if Lawnover was keeping a harem. He hadn't struck me as having that kind of energy. I found myself thinking about his secretary, but she was, if anything, even more unappetizing than he was. Daphne was pale and frail, but her features were regular. With exercise and a decent protein diet, she'd be cute—if she'd be a little more assertive.

I watched her out the door and spoke sternly to myself. Susan, you're not running the world. Rosa Puertas is the problem now, do what you can where you have the means. As I got up, I turned to see Lawnover's secretary watching me across the dining room. That's why Daphne left. If I called her at home, I thought, and then said, Down, girl. One problem at a time. I wondered whose name the house was in. Maybe Lawnover's mother. He looked like a mamma's boy.

Mrs. Scott directed me to the Urban Studies Center, "where the grant should have stayed." Mrs. Scott had never before offered any comment about the running of Benson. When I got to the Center, a small suite of rooms on the ground floor of an old classroom building, I walked into an empty office to find Diane Sampson pacing back and forth in the unlit rooms.

She stopped in her tracks like a tigress when she saw me, her face contorted in a scowl that turned to sunshine when she recognized me.

"Susan Soulperson!" she said, coming up to take my hand in both of hers to give me some pumps. "Come on in. That Keeney chick said you were out of the office and she didn't know where. She's not into sisterhood with you. Tell you something else. I can read your mind."

"I know you can, and it seems everybody else can, too. Naomi's back and I guess she's staying with you."

Diane leaned against the table and began to nod slowly. I went on. "I have to see her. I've decided to go over this case from the beginning. There's something we're not seeing, and I'm convinced it's something Naomi knows."

Diane flashed expressions across her face like semiphore signals, excited, sad, excited again.

"All right! I been telling her that. But it's doing no good. She says it's the CIA on her case. I don't know what they said to her on the phone, but she wants to drop the complaint and drop you. She's staying at my place till she gets everything turned off. Then she wants to cut out, never to be seen again. I told her she couldn't take off without saying something to you, but she says if they could figure she was at your daddy's pad, they can find her anywhere. I made her stay home at my place, so she's in my spare bedroom with the covers pulled over her head."

Finding Naomi at an unlisted number across the country seemed like using an atomic bomb to shoot a rabbit, and I couldn't understand what Naomi could know about the project that I didn't already have in hand. I decided Diane ought to know it too—in case something happened to me. That's how you can get caught up in intrigue, I guess.

"Diane, I found out that some of those EC project classes are just moonshine. That can't be what she knows. Rosa Puertas and my secretary are both evidence of that."

While I gave Diane the details, her eyes began to flash. She put up her hand like a policeman and reached for her phone.

"Don't waste it on me, Sooze. I'm calling the main man, Dr. Henderson. It's time we rang the Avon bell in his ivory tower."

Ron Henderson and Harriet Guyon were the only scholars at Benson I'd heard of before arriving. He'd made quite a splash several years back with a much reprinted article called "Doing the Undoable," a toughly thought out presentation of what could and couldn't work in attacking inner-city problems. Since then he'd brought out a number of short pieces that caused a lot of rethinking of traditional ideas about welfare.

When Diane led me into his cluttered office, I knew why she stayed at Benson when almost every week brought her an offer to go elsewhere. It was the way she looked at him, not his appearance. He was a middle-aged, middle-class West Indian who was going bald. He seemed mild and distracted, but his eyes gave the show away. He saw us and he also saw, not what we were, but what we could be.

He looked like an El Greco saint, but his voice told that despite his hopes for the future, he had a clear grasp of what was happening right now.

"Diane says you're all right. That'll do for me, Ms. Meredith. Something's troubling both of you, so talk away," he said, lifting stacks of IBM printout to uncover some chairs and taking one himself.

He was direct, and that's a saintly virtue.

"Dr. Henderson, the Education Continuation project has turned into some kind of swindle. It's not providing its students with the promised training, and I'm convinced there's some kind of financial fiddling going on. I understand the grant was a result of your proposal. Why aren't you running it?"

"Why should I?" he asked comfortably and I recalled that saints are often difficult to live with. "I'm a scholar, not an administrator. I think I'm closing in on a set of ideas about the mechanics of social change. I believe that's more important than running a pilot project for a few hundred people. Administrators are a dime a dozen. What's involved in running a project? Answer your mail and listen to complaints. Personally, I thought Diane would have made a better administrator than Cartwright, but we have agreed that neither of us would interfere with the other's problems."

Diane smiled at me in a way that was clearly habitual.

"He was afraid he'd get too dependent on me," she said fondly. He went on as if she'd said nothing, although his next words were a comment on what she had said.

"In our separate ways, we're apparently a little intimidating. We'll leave this place as soon as we get an offer from an institution big enough to be able to cope with both of us. But to return to your question," he said and paused for a good thirty seconds.

"He's on another plane," said Diane, showing me the space between her front teeth. I couldn't believe it. He was treating her as if she were anybody, and she seemed to love it. Then I saw the attraction. He wasn't threatened by her. He started up again as if there'd been no interruption.

"If I left the project, I really shouldn't be trying to second guess what's being done, should I? But you say the instruction isn't appropriate. How?"

I went into detail, pulling together everything I'd heard from Harriet Guyon and Rosa Puertas, finishing up with my story about Gloria Keeney.

"If I hadn't been in higher education so long, I'd say that your story is incredible. But what kinds of jobs are they training for? The proposal was clearly for vocational-technical and the resulting middle management skills, not a baccalaureate program."

He was the calmest man I'd met in years. I was regaling him with a story of how *his* project had been wrenched out of shape and he talked about it as if it were happening to someone else.

"Don't you feel any responsibility? Your reputation as a scholar will suffer if these things keep on."

He smiled as if I'd promised chocolate cake for dessert.

"Those who know me, will know it wasn't my fault. Those who don't aren't entitled to an opinion."

Diane was watching me, and though her face was absolutely blank, I could tell that she was having a fine time watching me flounder with this man who seemed so mild and at the same time was so impregnable. I tried again.

"Do you think the changes they made in the program are to make money?"

He looked judicious.

"This isn't a large project. With only a couple of million spread over four years it isn't important money. Certainly it's not enough to risk jail time. Most of the dollars go for participant support and faculty time. Besides, the foundation's controls are pretty tight. I designed them myself."

He stopped and looked at a blackboard that was covered with equations. I didn't need to be told he wanted to get back to work, so I fired one more shot before he left us for that higher plane again.

"I know a man who explains all crime as motivated by either love or money."

I'd managed to get his attention. Henderson was into generalizations, so I gave him some problems.

"Cartwright's a homosexual, but he claimed Naomi turned him on. You say there's not enough money in the grant to cause larceny, but they beat her up and threatened her across the country to make her drop her case. How's that for a problem, Dr. Henderson? Are you sure there's no money they could get?"

He'd picked up a sheaf of printout and was staring at the aggregation sheet, but the paper flew from his hands like a startled pheasant.

"They've done what!" he exploded.

Diane put a restraining hand on his shoulder.

"Ron, darling. I wish you'd listen sometimes when I talk to you. I told you about that at breakfast. Why did you think Naomi was staying with us?"

His dark face took on a reddish tinge and he pulled the corners of his mouth down.

"She knows something she doesn't know she knows," he announced like a Delphic oracle. "Let's talk to her."

Once I had his attention, Ron Henderson was no longer the absent-minded professor. I saw what Diane saw in him, a dynamo that had only to be turned on. He made three phone calls and left instructions that they were to be returned to Diane's home phone and took off with Diane in pursuit as if there weren't enough minutes in the hour to do what had to be done.

Cartwright, on the other hand, had all the time in the world. The first time I'd been to see him, he'd had a lawyer present and his replies had been checked with the lawyer and then had emerged as monosyllabic and not at all informative. Today, he felt very confident. He was in his shirt sleeves working at some kind of lettering project that filled his entire executive desk with pens and brushes, and all sorts of piles of paper and ink bottles. He even had a lighted magnifying glass mounted to give additional light to a viewing board.

"I'm right in the middle of something, Susan. Why don't you take a look at the letter to the editor of the student paper while I finish up this piece? It'll only take a minute."

I wondered why he so openly pursued his hobby during working hours, but I took the newspaper after he told me it demonstrated what happened when Affirmative Action went too far. Since I had a lot of trouble making AA go *anyplace*, I was willing to read.

The letter got my attention fast:

> The Editor:
>
> The recent demise of two members of the WASPMALE Establishment on this campus indicates the structural contradictions of this institution. While alive, they were the symbols of economic and penile oppression of minorities, women, and the developing third world. Dead, nothing has changed, as the appointment of the Imperialist Lackey, Dr. Marvin Davers, confirms. As Box and Cox and Box again of the oppressive infrastructure, the puppets are interchangeable and will remain so until the masculine-military-industrial-technological oppression is finally ended by the authors of these deeds by the executive release arm of the Parthenogenesis Party. All Power to the Great Mother!
>
> Name Withheld By Request

"That's what happens when the government gets involved in everything," he informed me.

I studied his reddish face. Booze, not exposure to the elements had done that. He looked away.

"What was it you wanted, Miss Meredith?"

Even across the room I could smell the fruity odor of alcohol on his breath. If he wasn't at full efficiency, I might make him reveal something.

"The EC project you're running is in trouble. Lawsuits are in prospect and questions have been raised about the way money has been spent on the project."

Cartwright's face blanched under his network of broken capillaries. The skin around his lips went white.

"If this is another so-called Affirmative Action case, Miss Meredith, I want my lawyer present."

I had never enjoyed smiling quite so much as I did when I told him it was standard litigation for a failure to perform a contract. Cartwright opened and closed his mouth with an audible clack. Dry mouth time. I pressed on and sketched in what Rosa Puertas had told me. When I finished, I was startled to see that Cartwright had recovered his poise. He picked up his pencil and sighted along it.

"That kind of litigation never comes to anything except lawyer's fees. Any non-performance was on her part, not ours."

He touched the intercom switch.

"You said the woman's name was Rosa Puertas? Let's take a look at her transcript."

When the secretary brought the Puertas file in, Cartwright put on a pair of glasses and cleared his throat while he peered at the sheaf of papers. After a while he said Hum! and stared into the middle distance. Finally, he turned ponderously in my direction.

"Susan, this is a serious situation. I believe the woman has misrepresented her previous education. I don't think Mrs. Puertas can have much of a case. Even her grades seem inadequate. Thank you for warning us, but one of our double-check loops had already caught the error. Well?"

I wasn't ready to go, since Rosa Puertas had shown me transcripts which featured straight A's. Besides, Cartwright sounded as if he were improvising.

"Could I see the transcript, please?"

Cartwright smiled again. This time he looked smug. He was a fool but he wasn't stupid.

"But you said this wasn't an Affirmative Action case, Susan. I'm afraid I can't. Need to know, and all that."

He tossed the transcript into the central drawer of his desk and picked up his pen.

"Are you into calligraphy, Susan?" he asked.

For the third president of Benson University within two weeks, Davers was in excellent humor. Although Motley was rooted in one of the chairs before the presidential desk looking serious, Davers was laughing as I came in the door. He took off his glasses to wipe his eyes and then stared at me with his face still crinkled from smiling.

"If I accomplish nothing else, Susan, I will have saved us from a first amendment encounter between the police and the student paper. You've seen the letter about Barker and Tate? It's obviously a joke, a sick one, I can say as the one occupying the hot seat. But I could see this thing developing, the editor trying on a Peter Zenger costume, the district attorney pleading the common good, and nobody looking at the letter. Thank God I'm a political scientist. The letter's a hodge-podge of ancient slogans from every part of the political spectrum from Bakunin to the ultra-Montanists."

He paused expectantly, and it made me nervous. I had the feeling that someplace in this conversation there was going to be bad news.

"It seemed a little odd," I said, wondering what Motley was here for.

"It's a lot odd," Davers said, "so I didn't ask the editor who wrote the letter, I told him. It had been signed, 'Name Withheld by Request.' Motley here didn't think it was funny."

Davers stared at me and his face lost definition. "You don't, either, I guess. Well, you wanted to see me?"

I didn't really feel comfortable discussing the EC project in front of Motley, so I started at the other end. "Naomi Wilson is back in town," I said. "Whoever's been harassing her traced her all the way to my father's house. I think since we agree about her situation, you don't have to take anything to the board. You can have her reinstated with all her back pay. That's within your prerogatives."

Davers looked from me to Motley and then back again and I knew there was going to be bad news.

"Susan," he said and then inserted a pause that told me a lot. "I don't think Naomi Wilson has been pursuing this case wholeheartedly. Here she made a complaint last spring, and then she wanders off, takes another job, and leaves the state. Now you say she's back. I'll have to have an attorney's opinion as to whether or not her case is live."

There were about seven flaws in what he said, but this was no time for debate.

"When the AA office takes up the complaint, it's live till the officer says it isn't. Call all the lawyers you want. I've made a request that this go on the agenda of the next board meeting, and if you want HEW enforcing the request, try to keep it off."

I turned to Motley. "Part of the delay has been by this institution, I've decided, because Naomi knows something about the EC project that nobody wants aired. I've already found out a number of things and I have other investigators working."

Motley took out another of his long, pencil-thin cigars and examined it. When he spoke, it wasn't to me but to Davers.

"She's just talking. Sound and fury."

"How about Rosa Puertas? She's going to sue Benson for failure to perform a contract. How about a senior in sociology who doesn't recognize the names of Riesman, Durkheim, or Mills? Dr. Henderson is checking things through, and so is Harriet Guyon."

When I mentioned Harriet Guyon, Davers flinched visibly. I kept on.

"But inadequate contact time for credits given and an unqualified faculty are only the start. There's the matter of the managing of finances. It looks like embezzlement on a grand scale and the state auditors have some questions they want to ask Mr. Cartwright."

The last was a spontaneous inspiration that I regretted immediately, though it brought Motley to his feet. There was something about the money aspect of the grant that made everybody nervous.

"It's been interesting to listen to this nonsense, Davers," Motley said. "But this little skirt thinks she's got a case; she has one, but it's against herself for defamation of character. I'm going to warn Cartwright to hire a lawyer. See you in court, sweetcheeks."

He left in a blue swirl of strong-smelling cigar smoke. Davers stared at me across the expanse of his desk and steepled his fingers. He was trying to look presidential, but the impression was of a man close to tears.

"Susan, Motley was blackmailing me. He has witnesses to put me on the floor where Tate was found."

I didn't want to believe what I was hearing.

"*You* didn't kill him?"

Davers shrugged. "I might as well have. Mrs. Scott heard us arguing about the Project and then I stormed out of his office. I went into the men's room to recover my poise and when I came out a few minutes later, I found him at the foot of the stairs from his private entrance and I knew I'd be suspected immediately. I went back to my office and started making phone calls so I'd have an alibi."

I felt the small hairs on the back of my neck start lifting up.

"But no one knew he hadn't died of a stroke or something until the autopsy."

Davers made an ineffectual gesture with his hand. "I tell you I found him. I figured he'd fallen on the stairs, but people would think I pushed him."

"Didn't Mrs. Scott see you leave his office?"

Davers looked even more ready to cry.

"She was gone when I left Tate's office."

"How do you know she heard your argument?" I asked before it dawned on me I was asking cornering questions of a man who may have been a killer.

Davers took out his handkerchief.

"While we were arguing our loudest, she buzzed in to tell the president she was going to lunch." He looked sheepish. "She's an excellent secretary. It was probably a way to tell us we were being overheard. She saw me enter, she heard me argue, but she didn't see me go. And," he said, so I could understand the hopelessness of his situation, "Mrs. Foss, the receptionist, is on sick leave so there was no other witness around."

He blew his nose for a long time and then looked out the window, his most characteristic gesture. I wondered if I was looking at a murderer and decided I wasn't.

"If Motley said he had a witness, it was probably himself. Since you didn't do it, Motley killed him."

Davers sighed from his shoetops.

"Gloria Keeney was his witness. I think he has something going with her, and she'll do whatever he says. I guess I'm sunk."

"No, sir," I told him energetically, trying to lift him up. "You tell Lieutenant Bliss right away. I'm sure he'll understand," I said grandly, though I wasn't positive that he wouldn't arrest Davers immediately. "Do you want me to tell him?"

Davers began to breathe as if he'd just run a mile. He sat down and stared at his blotter.

"Would you? If you explain it, maybe he won't jump to conclusions."

"What made Tate so angry?" I asked.

"I didn't know at the time, but after I was named acting president, Motley came in and began to tell me about the project. He made no bones about the fact that it was a swindle, but he said that unless I shut up, Benson would have a terrible mess and wouldn't get another grant ever. I—um—was playing for time when I said I wasn't going to support you on the Wilson case. A project like that can ruin a university's reputation for decades. And he had me, Tate, and Barker all implicated. Somehow he had our signatures on all sorts of documents and policy statements. That, plus his threat to accuse me of Tate's murder really shut me down."

He stopped to search my face.

"If it had been just the murder of Tate, I think I could have stood it, but this made it look as if I'd murdered Tate to hide my thefts from the project, and that was unsupportable."

He stared at me a long time.

"You do believe me, don't you, Susan?"

I had till he began telling me all this.

"What are you going to do about Motley and Bronterre and Cartwright?" I asked.

He sketched determination on his face.

"I'm going to fire the boogers. All of them. But the first thing I'm going to do is reinstate Naomi Wilson, with back pay. Then I'll go to see Lieutenant Bliss and tell him everything."

He walked around the desk to take my hands and he was staring into my eyes in the strangest way. Just then, the phone buzzed. Without releasing my hand or taking his eyes off mine, he reached for the phone. He put on his presidential face as he answered, but it dissolved when he spoke.

"It's for you. Lieutenant Bliss."

I was trying to decide why Davers was acting so strangely when Harry's voice came on.

"Susan, I have bad news."

"It's Naomi?" I asked, my voice husky with apprehension that tightened my throat. We hadn't been able to keep her safe.

"She's gone. It's Diane Sampson."

It was as if someone had cut the strings that kept my knees stiff and I sank back against the desk. Davers was staring at me again. In about a second I was going to sob.

"What happened to her?"

"She's in trouble. When she and Henderson got to her apartment, Naomi was gone and she saw Bronterre getting into a car."

He sighed like a wind coming down a chimney.

"Susan, she didn't wait for words or anything. She beat the living juice out of him. Fortunately for Bronterre, a cruiser saw it and broke it up. Unfortunately for Diane, they thought she was a prostitute beating up on a john and Henderson was her mac, even though he was trying to stop her. Bronterre's going to file charges. Can you put her in touch with a lawyer? I can't."

"What was Bronterre doing there?" I shrieked. "You know Naomi had been threatened by those people."

"I don't know who threatened her," Harry said with an edge on his voice. "Bronterre had a perfectly good explanation. He says you and he had discussed a compromise about Naomi on Friday night and he wanted to see if he could talk Naomi into accepting it."

"How did he know she was back?" I asked.

"He says he didn't know she was gone. When he didn't find her at home, he said he assumed she'd be staying with a friend and he figured Diane Sampson would be it. He says he rang the doorbell, received no answer and walked in when he saw the door was ajar. Naomi was gone and he was leaving when Diane arrived."

I listened to the noise along the wire for a while.

"Susan, we're having to hold Diane for disorderly

conduct. I had the charge reduced from Assault and Battery. It didn't make Bronterre very happy and he's threatening all sorts of legal suits. She needs a lawyer."

"What about Ron Henderson?" I asked. "What's he charged with?"

"One of the arresting officers knew him so they let him go. He took off as if his shirt was on fire, but he hasn't gotten her a lawyer."

"I'll do that, Lieutenant."

"Don't call me that," he barked.

"Lieutenant, I have here Dr. Davers. He has some things to tell you that will change your mind on lots of topics."

Bliss said a *baaaad* word. "Don't hang up yet, Susan. Can he hear me?"

Davers had moved off and was looking out the window again. I nodded and then said yes into the phone.

"Leave the office immediately you put him on the phone. I think there's at least a sixty percent chance he killed Tate."

Nine

After that, there wasn't much left to say. I handed the phone to Dr. Davers, who squeezed my hand as he took it and began—unpromisingly, I thought—with "Things are very complicated here." I went out to phone Bob Mercer from the call director on Mrs. Scott's desk and arranged to meet him at the police station. When I told him who we were going to see, he was immediately interested. Maybe things were not too busy at Legal Services because we met in a dead heat at the front door of the downtown station.

The lobby held the kind of silence that follows a lot of noise, so when Mercer asked the desk sergeant about Diane Sampson, I wasn't surprised to hear that she had been released about five minutes before. It seemed Bronterre had changed his mind about making charges.

Mercer wasn't troubled about losing a client, but he had wanted to meet Diane.

"Win some, lose some. Buy you a cup of coffee? I ought to pay you finder's fees. Had a gal come in, said you turned her life around. Filed for divorce and the other woman was her sister-in-law. How's that for American gothic? Anyway, I wanted Diane's autograph. If volleyball ever makes it to TV, she'll be a star."

I hadn't been paying much attention because it was time to have things out with Gloria Keeney, and I wasn't looking forward to it.

"I'll try for an autograph, Bob. Really," I told him after I explained that I had a sort of guy now. "I have a lot to do today," I said, not recognizing dramatic irony when I spoke it. But where was Naomi?

Gloria had taken a long lunch hour to get her hair tinted, and the overhead fluorescents picked up the metallic dyes, giving her some surrealistic purple highlights. She seemed to like it, though, primping in a hand mirror while she talked to someone on the phone.

"Here she comes now," she said. I don't like quarreling with a sister, but as Daniel Derbyshire says, sisterhood without obligation is a nothing relationship. I decided we'd better have it out right then, but she put down the phone and began.

"I think you should know, Susan, that I've applied for a transfer to the EC project office. I haven't felt comfortable here—and with you holding down the top job, there's no place for me to advance. I really can't do my best when my supervisor feels threatened by me. I'm sure you'd be happier with a different secretary, an ethnic perhaps," she ended, drawing her mouth into an ugly shape as she stressed ethnic.

Then she was talking again, as if she had a number of topics to bring up before I could interrupt. "I have a chance to get on the executive track over there. Then I can come in at any hour and have long lunches with handsome policemen."

There were a lot of things to say, but I wasn't going to say them under the circumstances.

"I'd like you to come into my office, Gloria. There are a few things we have to go over," I said and marched into my room. Gloria was at least ten years older than I, and I'd need all the authority I could muster if I was going to get any information out of her.

As she dawdled in the outer office, I made notes of what I was going to cover. If she wanted a positive recommendation—a requirement when any assignment is changed by promotion or transfer—she'd have to be on good behavior for the rest of the week.

The phone rang in the outer office and I picked it up the same time Gloria did. Since she'd been short-stopping my calls, I wasn't surprised when Eleanor Barker said, "Susan! I've been trying to reach you for days!"

Another example of Gloria's work. This sounded like personal animosity rather than anything else. I wondered what she wanted as Gloria came on the line.

"Thank you, Gloria, I have it," I said. Then I waited for her to hang up. She didn't until I repeated my words. Then came a reluctant click. "Now, Eleanor, how have you been?"

I didn't make any reference to Motley's drugging me at the party because I didn't think she knew about it, but I couldn't have said a word anyway. She began to talk in her compulsive way, the words tumbling out as if she were a girl reciting what happened at her first prom.

"Susan, my life has been an absolute *whirl* since Buzz passed on. I told you I was going to make a clean break with the past. So I sold all my furniture and moved into an apartment. I didn't really want to go back to the midwest. After all, my friends are here. And that's my news. I'm getting married. To a man! Tonight!"

I made my manners.

"That's exciting news. Do I know him, Eleanor?"

"Oh, yes. One of your close colleagues at the college. Roger. Roger Motley. You know, we've known each other since before Sarawak. And he was divorced simply ages ago, so there's no scandal. And Roger is so impetuous. He said it might seem soon to strangers, but the heart has its reasons, you know."

I tried to think of something appropriate to say, but Eleanor didn't need any assistance.

"To make a long story short, we're flying out to Las Vegas in the Jolly Roger this evening. We're all going, the old East of Sarawak bunch. I almost wish Buzz was here to come along. He'd be so happy for me."

Not for the first time, I wondered how strong a hold on reality Eleanor had.

"That certainly sounds like fun," I heard myself saying. Well, what else could I say? "All best wishes, Eleanor. And let me know when you get back to town. I'll want to give you a wedding present."

"There is one thing more, Susan," said the inconsequential voice on the phone. "Buzz has a message for you."

I thought for a moment that Eleanor had graduated from gin to something more exotic, but I waited to see what the message was.

"I was going through his things before sending them off to the Goodwill and found a big package addressed to you, Susan Meredith, the Affirmative Action officer. It looks like a report, or something."

It probably ticks, I thought, remembering the ghendo seeds. She'd known nothing about that, I was sure, but then I thought things through as Eleanor continued to rattle. Barker was part of the East of Sarawak crowd, and I didn't believe that Motley had killed him to get Eleanor. Whatever was going on, they'd been in it together. Therefore, the package was one more trick of Motley's. He wanted to get me someplace and the package was the lure. Eleanor began to run down, so I put in a question.

"When can I come by for the package, Eleanor? You must have a thousand things to do. Where did you say you were living?"

"Oh, I won't be there. I'm getting fitted for my

going-away dress and then I have to have my hair done, but I'll be free about six-forty-five. Tell you what, Susan. We're leaving from the Correles Airport at seven, you know, the one out on Coors Boulevard? Roger's been keeping the Jolly Roger there because there's less traffic. Anyway, we can have one last drink in memory of our good times at Benson University. Roger's decided to leave the academy. He wants to write a book. He says he intends to expose higher education."

That was new information I thought Harry would like to know. After a few more bubbles and burbles, she hung up. Women like that puzzle me. They obviously need a man around to function at all, and when they're without one, there's always another man ready to pick up the traces dropped by the last one. Then I got serious. Eleanor was forty pounds overweight, had the mind of a mosquito, and drank like a wino. If Roger Motley saw something in her, it was an advantage to him. Any other explanation would get to a liberated woman's poise.

So the whole gang was taking off tonight and Motley wanted me in the area, too. I wondered if I should phone Harry with this news. I'd think the police would like to know when a number of people associated with a murder all left town at once.

Gloria cleared her throat ostentatiously. I'd been thinking over Eleanor's phone call and hadn't noticed her come in.

"You said you wanted to see me, Susan. Here I am. Let's get this over," she began combatively, which was just as well because I was going to land on her hard.

"Please sit down, Gloria," I said, not liking what I was going to do. "This is an exit interview. Today is Thursday, and you needn't come in again this week.

Before I write up your recommendation, there are some things that only you can tell me."

Gloria shifted in her seat. She had a pretty good idea what was coming next. "We haven't gotten along too well, Miss Meredith, but I think as sisters, we have to put personalities aside, don't you?" she asked, putting the ball in my court.

"Exactly," I told her. "Now, my questions. Why have you been shortstopping my calls? Why couldn't Rosa Puertas get through to me? Why have committee deliberations been leaked to outsiders? Those are my first questions."

I held up a stopping hand when she started to answer. "I don't think you want to answer those questions now, so I'm going to ask you something else first."

She didn't blush, but her face was pinker than when she'd sat down. I didn't think she was much more than a tool being used by people a lot smarter than she, so I wanted her to know she was in real trouble.

"Here's the question. Can you identify C. Wright Mills? Emile Durkheim? David Riesman?"

Her face grew more composed with each name. When I finished, she was ready and I was embarrassed when I heard what she said.

"Those are members of our sociology department. We wrote a memo to them the other day, or don't you remember?"

She was going to wish she hadn't been gratuitously mean in a moment. I picked up the Benson catalogue and slid it across the desk. "You can look in the faculty roster and you won't find one of them. That ought to tell you you have a serious problem, one you don't even know you have."

Gloria had a lot of natural composure. As far as she was concerned, I hadn't laid a glove on her yet. I wished there were an easier way to do this, but Gloria had been betraying me right along.

"I examined your transcripts from the EC project, Gloria. You're within a semester of graduating in sociology, but you didn't recognize one of those names, names that even a freshman in the field should know. Each of them has written a number of books, and all of them are a part of any sociology curriculum. You haven't read any of their work or apparently even heard of them."

Gloria examined the flawless finish on her fingernails. "I—don't have a very good memory. I remember them now."

I didn't ask her to name a book one of them had written. My aim wasn't to make her ridiculous but to show her that there was too much she didn't know. "You should have let those calls from Rosa Puertas come through, Gloria. She has the same problem you do. Her credentials don't mean a thing. I don't know what went on in that project, but professional training it wasn't."

Gloria was intelligent. It was too bad she hadn't been educated. Her face turned from pink to white and she stared at me as if her eyes could burn holes in my face.

"I thought—" she began, and then stopped for a long moment. "Roger said—" and then she stopped again. That was all I had to hear, but she had started to talk now and it was like a dam breaking. "He said he would guarantee I'd be an executive when the plan was finished. I didn't even have to go to those mickey classes. All I had to do was keep an eye on you. I thought it was too easy. But Roger and I have an understanding. We're going off together and he's going to write a book."

Things began to fall into place. Motley was going to marry Eleanor Barker and he was going to write a book with her, too. I had the silly image of Gloria going along as a secretary. Then I got serious. I wondered if she'd been invited to the airport tonight the way I had.

"He tells that to all the girls," I said. "Eleanor Barker thinks she's going off to Las Vegas with him tonight to get married."

That got results. Gloria was on her feet immediately, her cheeks two bright spots. She'd thought she was manipulating Motley all the while he'd been using her.

"He isn't!" she said in a strangled voice.

I was still looking for the key to the whole EC project takeover.

"Did you have to kick back on the support fees from the project?"

Gloria was still thinking about Motley's betrayal, and she shook her head abstractedly. "No. That was the big plus. You put in three hours a week and you got the equivalent of a full-time salary. It was gravy. You don't think he can possibly prefer her to me, do you?"

Even though I'd never liked her, it was painful to watch sexual jealousy eat away at her composure. Then I recalled that Bronterre had dropped charges so he wouldn't have to appear in court tonight. Maybe all the pirates were leaving at once. That meant they'd completed the sacking of Benson University. I still didn't have any hard evidence of their wrongdoing.

"He'll be at the Correles Airfield tonight from six-forty-five till seven. Why don't you ask him? Tell him I sent you."

Without a word she spun on her heel. A second later, the outer door slammed behind her. Picking up a package, indeed! Motley now would know that I was closing in on his operation. Even if he managed to convince Gloria that she was number one, I'd learned enough to put holes in his operation. The one thing I still didn't know was why so much effort to steal such a relatively small amount. Nevertheless, I had enough evidence to take to Davers.

I had my hand on the phone to call Davers when Diane and Ron Henderson came in. She was radiant, but he looked as if he'd been caught stealing pies.

"What you want, we got. Right, Ron-hon?"

Henderson sighed and took off his topcoat, a hat, a muffler, and gloves. Then he dumped them on a chair and rubbed his hands together. Diane was wearing a lightweight pants suit and seemed as warm as toast. There were a lot of incongruities between these two, but from the look on Diane's face, Ron Henderson had what it took.

"Tell the girl, Ron. She's waiting to hear."

He sighed again and started in. "I feel like a fool. I told you I'd done all the financial checking. I had and I hadn't. I set up the reporting parameters because I didn't want some swift thinker diverting money from the grant. That didn't happen. Then I checked the state part. There's an in-kind contribution, and I made a mistake. I figured the larceny, if it came, would be from the grant. It was right here in the budget office."

He went off to another plane. Diane smiled fondly at him.

"He's working on a feedback loop that would catch it, even if everybody connected with the project and the school was bent. He'll be back in a minute."

"Got it!" Ron said. "OK. Nothing in the project at the lowest aggregation level, but at the university level, Bronterre was draining off full-time faculty equivalents for each of those graduate students who were in the program."

Both Diane and Ron were grinning at me as if they'd made a complete explanation of everything. "I give up," I told them. "What's that mean?"

"The graduate students were getting paid twice, but they didn't know it. And they wouldn't even begin to wonder till they got their W-4 forms in January and saw double Social Security payments. The salary dollars were kicked into the operations budget under Other Contractual Services and then transferred into the discretionary budget of the president. That's a holdover from the days when this was a private college and the local administration had a lot of discretion."

I still didn't quite understand what had happened, but Ron was looking pleased.

"I see how to keep this from happening again," he said and stared at the wall while I queried Diane with my eyes.

"It's a problem for him, that's all," she said. "What I want to know is where's Naomi and what did she see?"

I remembered Eleanor's call. Motley wanted me out at the suburban airfield. They were planning to abscond and they wanted to take me along. I recalled all the horrible stories about people being thrown out of airplanes without parachutes.

"She's at the Correles Airport. I think Bronterre took her there in the trunk of his car. They're going to run right now, tonight."

I turned to Ron who was starting to put on his coat, hat, muffler and gloves.

"Do you have any way of finding out if Bronterre has used his financial powers to write any checks or invest in bearer bonds?"

He stopped in mid-gesture, one arm half in a coat sleeve and began to think. Diane started to pull on his arm when he came to again.

"No!" he announced strongly. "We did that other stuff your way and all we got was arrested. Let me think a minute."

It took him a full minute, but when he smiled I knew he had an answer.

"Harvey Welles. He has to countersign any share order. We can ask him."

He slipped out of his topcoat and unbuttoned his suit coat and reached into an inside pocket to take out a memo book that had a clip lock on it. I wondered if Ron wore both a belt and suspenders. I'd have to ask Diane sometime. He riffled through the pages and began to punch up numbers on my call director.

"Hello, Harvey? This is Ron Henderson. Right! How are things with you? Well, I have a problem or I wouldn't be phoning you right now. Have you countersigned any legal instruments with Mr. Bronterre lately?"

I'm usually not excitable, but I heard my pulse in my ears. I saw that Diane was watching Ron as if he were going to move suddenly.

"You have—what were they? Oh, the usual fortnightly pay warrants. Nothing else in prospect either, right? Sorry to have troubled you, Harvey. Yes. I surely will. See you."

Ron put down the phone and began to pace. He hit his hand with his fist. "They can't be such fools as to take off with a measly half a million dollars."

Diane and I looked at each other, but then Ron had a different perspective. And then I thought about how much money it would take to bribe me. Let's see. Five hundred thousand divided among Motley, Cartwright, and Bronterre would be less than two hundred thousand apiece. If they'd been planning something with Barker, it would have been for more money than that. The interest on a chunk of money that small wouldn't pay for the gas Motley's C-47 burned, and Motley wasn't a small-time operator. Now, for a piece of money to bribe me, it would have to—

Diane and I both told Ron he was right at the same moment, and then we all started talking at once.

"We have to find Naomi!" Diane said.

"There's something that escapes me," Ron said softly.

"Hold it!" I announced like a drill sergeant. Diane and Ron stared at me. "We know that Barker supplied the academic respectability. Bronterre was the money man. Motley planned and led. What was Cartwright's contribution? He wasn't strong arm."

"He was a gopher and for laughs," Diane said. "He went for coffee."

"They were a country team," I went on. "Even Eleanor was a part. She knew languages. Motley wouldn't keep somebody around for nothing."

Ron started to speak when I saw it.

"He's the artist. He forged what had to be made up. I surprised him in his office with all his tools spread out. That's why they're leaving tonight. I bet they looted this place from attic to cellar."

"We can't prove that," Ron told me.

Diane slid off the desk where she had perched.

"Who needs proof? They take Naomi and she's *gone!*"

"And we'll be back in jail again if we try to stop them," Ron said despairingly as he started getting back into hat, coat, gloves, and muffler. "But if I expect to get any rest tonight—"

"Ron's right," I broke in. "These people have proved they're dangerous. If they have Naomi, it's because they intend to kill her. If they don't, we'll look like fools. In any case, we need police help."

Diane's face became mulish, but Ron looked relieved and began to nod. Halfway. I went on, knowing that I had to convince Diane.

"Look. I'll call Lieutenant Bliss and tell him what we think. He'll go out there ready for trouble and he'll have the resources and authority to stop them. How's that?"

I asked, picking up the phone. "He's as concerned as we are about Naomi."

I dialed while Diane and Ron talked in low tones. It took forever to complete the call. First it didn't ring, and then we were put on hold. If I'd been a Mary Roberts Rinehart heroine, I'd have made the meeting with Eleanor Barker and unmasked the criminals before Bliss and his troops arrived to keep the bad guys from killing me. But as I'd just convinced Diane, Motley's people wouldn't be impressed by the likes of us, even if Diane had black belts in all the martial arts.

Bliss was still talking to someone else when he picked up the phone. From the tone of his voice, he seemed angry, not at all the cool, in-charge policeman I'd known.

"I don't care what the judge says. Full surveillance. Get on it." His voice didn't modulate from the imperative tone as he went on to me. "Lieutenant Bliss here. What can I do to help you?"

Diane moved closer to hear the conversation, so I held the phone between us.

"I think you should do what's necessary to arrest three men. Motley, Bronterre, and Cartwright. They've been systematically looting money from Benson University. If you want proof, I can put Dr. Ron Henderson on the line."

"Susan," he said slowly, "this is the homicide detail. We don't cover white collar crime. Where are you?"

I heard Diane make a disgusted sound with her lips. Harry could be the most irritating man a liberated woman ever had to put up with, almost as bad as Ron Henderson, I reflected. Then I wondered why he wanted my whereabouts.

"In my office. I don't feel like an Italian meal, if that's what you're asking. You've changed the definition of white collar crime if it now includes hiring thugs to beat up women, kidnapping, and setting traps to kill them."

He'd covered the transmitter to say something to someone else. When he came on again, he sounded more like himself.

"Tell me."

"Eleanor Barker asked me to meet her to look at some mysterious document left by her husband just before she leaves town to marry Roger Motley tonight. The last time I responded to an invitation from her, I was drugged. I think he wants to stop me from investigating things any further. This time he might be more direct."

"Where's the meeting supposed to take place?"

"Out at the Correles Airport where he keeps his airplane."

He gave me some silence over the phone. For a man who had demonstrated how fast he could think, Bliss was taking his time.

"Good," he said. "I'm sending a man over to take you out there. If they have some idea of cutting up rough, he'll handle it."

"But what about Naomi? We think they have her."

"Forget about Naomi. We've just about got these murders worked out, but we don't want a bunch of amateurs screwing things up. You stay right where you are and you'll be all right."

Diane was no longer at my elbow. She and Ron had left. Suddenly, I was furious.

"Lieutenant Bliss, I'm not going anyplace with your man. You go. I have other things that are more important. Tell Eleanor Barker you'd like to marry her. Then she'll do anything you ask. She might even give you that document I have so much trouble believing in."

Then I hung up. He was all right, but sooner or later,

these macho men want to patronize you. "Stay right there," they say, "and I'll get back to you in the fullness of time." He could handle that Motley business. Besides, Diane and Ron were obviously on their way out there. I was going to see Davers with the notes Ron Henderson had come up with. Maybe some part of the police department might like to stop a crime in progress if Benson's president blew the whistle.

Davers was still in his office, so I told him I'd be right over and grabbed all of Ron Henderson's documentation, slamming the door behind me. I was halfway down the darkened stairs before I remembered what had happened to me the last time I was wandering around an empty office building. That was all over, I assured myself as I trotted down the dark flights.

As usual after five, the administration building was as quiet as a mausoleum. My footsteps echoed in the marble-faced entry hall as I made my way up the formal stone staircase to the mezzanine where the President's office surveyed the central campus and the athletic fields.

I stood at the top of the stairs for a moment looking out over Benson. Even if I am a faculty brat and tend to think of college campuses as extended front yards to play on, I felt a flash of sentiment. On a fall evening, when the students are inside, and the lights are on in the libraries and laboratories and faculty offices, even a brat feels that there's something worthy about the academic enterprise, even one as ordinary as Benson. Maybe it wasn't as rich in tradition and scholarship as an Ivy League college, but it was slowly building those traditions with people like Harriet Guyon and Ron Henderson. After all, as Daniel loved to point out, Harvard started as a seminary.

Then the lights began coming on in the student dorms. Even if it lacked a good deal in tradition, Benson had a lot of the world's goods passing through it. A decent art collection, ten thousand students, and a good-sized endowment. That had attracted Motley and his people. A lot of money and no expectation of the pirates who'd come to loot it. They'd been stopped, by luck as much as anything else.

The president's suite was still lit up. Mrs. Scott had gone, but the door to the president's office was open. I could see immediately that the picture of Tate's grandfather had been removed, and Davers's souvenirs of his years in Africa had taken the place of honor. Even as I looked, I knew that something was wrong, but I told myself it was all the apprehension I'd had about Motley and his people that had made me so jumpy.

Davers was leaning against the wall, looking out over the campus as I had been. At that same moment I noticed without really looking that one of the assegais was missing from the wall. In a coalescing split second I saw it was protrudng from Davers' back. The spear head had passed completely through his chest and was stuck in the plaster of the wall beside the window, holding Davers in that position.

The blood was a tiny patch around the spot where the spear had entered and I had the idiotic thought that if I pulled the spear out, he would be all right. I reached out to touch the spear even as I told myself that piercing weapons should not be removed, but my touch disturbed the equilibrium and Davers fell to the floor in a crumpled heap. Because of the sudden movement, I stifled a scream and instinctively grasped the spear. It came out in a spurt of blood as a cool draft played on the back of my neck.

I had done the most foolish thing imaginable. I stood

over a dead man with the weapon that killed him in my hands and a witness coming in the door.

Ten

I dropped the spear guiltily. I turned around to see Arnold Lawnover. His eyes were darting around the fishbowls of his glasses to take in the room, Davers, the spear—and me.

"Woman! You've killed Dr. Davers!"

"Don't be silly!" I said in a voice that at first didn't want to come out and then was louder than I'd intended. "I thought I'd help him by taking it out."

Lawnover was as stern as a Red Cross First Aid instructor.

"Never try to remove a piercing weapon. It's the only thing that restricts the bleeding. Stand aside, woman."

That was the second time in less than a minute that Lawnover had called me woman. He found this situation to his liking. Of course, after three murders, I hadn't been performing up to par myself. I picked up the phone.

"Don't touch anything!" he said in a peremptory tone. He obviously saw himself as a crisis manager. "Davers is dead and the police won't want anything moved. Here," he went on masterfully, "I'll phone. If I tell them I found you at the scene with the weapon in your hands, it might impress even Lieutenant Bliss."

All this was hard to take, but I had only myself to blame. Things do balance up. I'd been convinced that Lawnover had killed Barker. Now he was certain I'd speared Davers. Lawnover and I would obviously never get along. Probably something in our genes. I kept hold of the phone.

"Nobody put you in charge, Arnold," I told him as I dialed the emergency number. He brought out the worst in me. He gave up on the phone and squatted down to peer at Davers.

"He was impaled by that thing against the wall. He must have been looking out the window the way I've seen him do it a dozen times. Like all the other times, the murderer struck from behind," I said.

Lawnover gave me a sharp glance.

"You always seem to be in the vicinity, Miss Meredith."

The phone rang and rang at the other end. Emergency number, ho!

"I was at the board meeting when President Tate was killed," I said. Now I was trying to justify myself to Lawnover! "Where were you? You always seem to have an alibi."

It kept ringing. Lawnover looked as if he had smelled something bad. "I always have work to do, Miss Meredith. I don't seem to have the time available that you do. I came over here to see what was keeping Dr. Davers. We had an appointment to see Dr. Martin, Mr. de Montremonte, and Mr. Bronterre at the art museum about culling the collection."

Somebody finally picked up the phone and said "Emergency" in a bored voice.

"This is Susan Meredith. I want to report a murder. On the Benson Campus. President Davers. I found Dr. Davers stabbed with a spear in his office. Lieutenant Bliss will want to know. No, this is not a prank. You can verify this call by phoning the president's number."

Then somebody said, "I will, lady," and hung up.

Lawnover stood staring at me with his legs apart and

his hands on his hips. His lip jutted out beneath a dark frown.

"This situation is without precedent, Miss Meredith. These murders have absolutely deprived Benson of most of its high-level executives. Dr. Barker, Professor Tate, and now, Dean Davers."

Lawnover always sounded so know-it-all that he infuriated me.

"More than that," I said. "Don't expect Bronterre to meet you. He's trying to escape right now."

His mouth dropped open gratifyingly, so I told him some more after I checked the time with my watch.

"Just about now, the police ought to be rounding them up at the Correles Airport. They kidnapped Naomi Wilson. They planned to murder me and probably Eleanor Barker as well. They had some kind of plan to raid this college of its resources. By the time it was discovered, they'd have escaped to a country with no extradition."

Lawnover's response was predictable. Utter disbelief.

The phone rang and I picked it up to hand it to Lawnover, but he motioned it away. It was the emergency number and I confirmed the earlier message. The voice still sounded bored.

"We'll send a man out. Don't leave, miss."

I told him I had no intention of doing so and hung up. Lawnover was thinking hard. I decided to pay him back for his "How old *are* you, Miss Meredith" remark.

"I've been getting all kinds of signals that something was wrong with the EC project. I think that whole crew, from Barker down to Cartwright, are a bunch of crooks. It's odd that people like yourself who are centrally involved didn't have any idea of what was going on."

More expressions crossed Lawnover's face in five seconds than I would have thought possible. Finally, he settled on a confident expression. "I had some suspicions myself that I have already begun to act upon. Bronterre owes me a report for the finance committee on the performance of Benson's stock holdings. I've been wondering why it's late."

Sometimes it's nice to twist the knife.

"Arnold, I've already alerted Ron Henderson and he's found clear evidence of fiscal wrondoing in the EC project."

But Lawnover wasn't listening anymore. He stared out the window at the darkness that made it a mirror. When he turned back to me, his face was smoothed of concern.

"The only thing the trustees can do is name me as the acting president. All the other possible candidates lack any sort of administrative experience. I hadn't wished this to happen yet, but I believe I owe it to Benson."

I made my own face absolutely impassive. He set everyone's teeth on edge just by breathing, and he thought he had a future as a college president. Then I heard myself asking a question.

"Who are you going to inform that you're available for the assignment, Dr. Lawnover?" I asked, my voice drenched in saccharine syrup.

He gave the question the sober consideration it deserved.

"Larry Simmonds. He's the current chairman of the board. We've been quite good friends since my sister and I financed our house at his bank. I've been able to give him the straight dope on what's been happening at Benson on a number of occasions. We have a profitable relationship."

Lawnover was hopeless. Simmonds had been using him as an informant, and now Lawnover expected to be repaid by being named president. I almost asked who would be Simmond's toady if Lawnover became the chief college executive, but the phone rang before I could be so ill advised. They might just do it!

"Why don't you answer it?" Lawnover asked, full of his new stature.

It was Harry. "Susan," he said, "we caught Cartwright, but Eleanor Barker is dead. Naomi isn't here, and neither are Motley and Bronterre. There's a chance they might be coming your way. Stay where you are and lock yourself in. Don't open for anyone except the police, understand?"

Harry's take-charge ways had irritated me before, but when he told me to do exactly what I wanted to, that was all right.

"All right," I said with a quaver in my voice that surprised me. I was about to tell him that I had Arnold Lawnover with me but he'd hung up already. Lawnover I could have handled as the murderer, but Motley was scary. I remembered how he'd manhandled me when I'd been drugged. I turned to Lawnover.

"The presidential murders are solved. Motley killed Eleanor Barker this evening. He escaped the police and Bliss thinks he might be coming back here. He said to lock everything and wait for the police. Do you want to phone home and say you'll be late? We'll be safe here."

Then I thought about what I had just said. Some liberated femme!

"Arnold, I didn't say you were here with me. Why don't you go on home, nobody would know."

Lawnover looked absolutely astonished and began to shake when I said that Motley had killed Eleanor Barker. I didn't feel too robust myself, especially if I was willing to be locked in a room with Arnold Lawnover. I took hold of myself. Emmaline Pankhurst! I said to myself to insert some starch into my backbone. Mary Wollstonecraft! George Sand!

"Why don't you go on?" I heard myself saying

casually. "There's no need to stay out of a sense of chivalry. Besides, I have a lot of things to think over."

Lawnover put on an expression I'd never seen on his face before. He was looking doggy, as if I'd finally come to my senses and perceived what a devil of a fellow he was. At that instant I would have swapped him for Motley, even up. I hoped he couldn't read the expression on *my* face.

"I'll lock the outer door, Susan. You lock the hallway," he said, marching off like a soldier. It only took me a second to snap the lock on the hall door. I turned around to see that I'd forgotten all about Dr. Davers. He was still lying on the floor. I looked up. Arnold Lawnover stood in the doorway trying to touch the lintel of the door. He had his back to me, but his neck was beet red.

A second later, I didn't feel too happy myself when I saw that Motley was backing him into the office, making small gestures at him with a chromium revolver. Motley looked happy when he saw me. Then he took in the body of President Davers and did an elaborate double-take.

"Education at Benson is something else! You people scarf up presidents like they were peanuts. And little Miss Equal Opportunity! Some days you can't lose for winning. What happened, sweetie? He was going to back you about that Wilson chick. Did he change his mind again?"

Lawnover was standing between us with his arms thrust straight toward the ceiling. Motley put the pistol in his pocket and shook his head disgustedly at Lawnover.

"For goodness sake, Lawnover, put your arms down. You didn't hear me say Simon Says Hands Up, did you?"

Arnold thought it over before he brought his hands

down. I noticed that he looked all in, as if he'd been running since breakfast. I didn't feel too steady myself. Motley seemed totally at ease as he inspected Davers.

"I was going to take him with me. Well, Susan." He turned to Lawnover. "But you're a problem, Fatty. I'll get back to you." He looked at me. "Was it a student or an alum that did that to him? The football season's barely started. OK. Let's get to work. Where are the keys to the president's car, Lawnover? In his pocket?"

Arnold shuddered with his whole body and began to express negatives in head shakes and stutters. I wondered why Motley was pretending he hadn't killed Davers.

"Get hold of yourself!" Motley ordered disgustedly. "You don't see sweetcheeks going to pieces, do you? Where are they?"

Lawnover's quavering arm pointed at Mrs. Scott's desk. "The central drawer. Are you going to make me a hostage?"

Motley stared at him as if he were difficult to take seriously.

"For an egghead, Lawnover, you watch a lot of TV. What do you think you're worth? This charmer and I are going to motor off into the night, but you I don't need."

Motley stopped to stare at the crumpled heap that was Davers and then turned to me.

"Don't even think about it, sweetpants. The outer door is locked and I shortstopped your call to the boys in blue."

There'd been something about that voice on the phone that was familiar. Motley winked and changed his voice. "I will, lady," he said and then motioned me back into the office. "You lie down on that couch and take your shoes off. I'm not casting today, but you won't run far without shoes, and I don't want to worry about you while I put Lawnover away."

I could feel the blood leach out of my face. There was no way I'd lie down while he killed Lawnover. His next words reassured me.

"There's this nifty store room between this office and the reception area, Lawnover. You're going into it. It's part of the old building and it's soundproof even though it opens onto an elevator shaft. You can stay there or you can try to slide down the cables. It's only about forty feet, but I'd advise you to stay in the room and yell now and again. They ought to pick up on you by tomorrow morning at least."

Motley turned to me again. "I said lie down."

Lawnover and I exchanged glances. I'd have run for the door, but Arnold didn't have an ounce of fight in him. He turned away toward the store room door. Motley encouraged him with a shove and Arnold stepped inside. Before I could scream, Motley took the pistol out of his pocket and fired. The shot, muffled by the storeroom, sounded no louder than a slap, but I heard the unmistakable sound of a falling body.

"Now you won't have any light in there, Lawnover, but you're not afraid of the dark, are you?" He turned to me. "He fainted. You don't take orders very well, do you? All right, take off your shoes. Now!"

I slipped my shoes off. I'd heard about foot fetishists, but I'd thought Motley had other concerns. Be serious, Susan, I told myself, this man has killed and will kill you if you cross him. If I could delay him until Harry arrived—but Motley spoke again.

"I was here before you arrived, sweetheart. I was ready to believe you'd poked a hole in old Davers after our interview earlier today and I was pretty sore. I intended to take him as a hostage, but now I'll take you."

"How did you manage to pick up my call to the

police?'' I asked, trying to think of a topic that might delay him. He was rummaging in Mrs. Scott's desk and finally found the keys.

"There's a central call director for the whole floor down the hall. One of my economies has been to shut down the twenty-four-hour service, remember? We're on automatic from six p.m. till seven a.m. Well, time to go. No, we'll leave your shoes here, Susan. I understand you're a jogger and I smoke too many cigars."

"You realize the police are looking for you and they've already caught Cartwright."

It was old news to him.

"You forgot I heard the romantic Lieutenant Bliss tell you to lock yourself in. Lawnover will give him the details when he finally arrives—after we've gone. Don't you want to say I'll never get away with this?"

"They already have your plane and they caught Cartwright. Eleanor is dead. Did you kill her?"

He sighed.

"Eleanor had a lot of problems, one of them was hypertension. Everything else worked out the way it was planned. The whole university had an eye on Cartwright and the EC project. You were very helpful in keeping everybody's attention on it. Cartwright doesn't have many needs. All he wanted was half a million."

I began to have a clear idea of the size of Motley's enterprise.

"Bronterre did the real stealing," I said.

"Right church, wrong pew, my dear. Bronterre's interested in objects of art, not money. He's been working a swindle with the Benson art collection."

"Then Barry Martin was right," I said more to myself than to him.

"Not quite, but you're getting warm. You already know the answer to the next question, what did I want—money, lots of it. And now I have it. You play your cards right and you can help me spend it."

"Ron Henderson knows it too, and you don't have him along. He said the EC money wasn't enough to attract all of you. he also knows that Cartwright forged Harvey Welles's signatures. What did you do, convert the endowment fund holdings into bearer bonds?"

Motley pocketed the keys and stared at me assessingly. He rounded his lips in a soundless whistle.

"You're something else, sweetie. We're getting out of here just in time. You'd have blown the whistle on us in another day or so. Tell you what. I don't like unwilling hostages."

He stopped and stared at me.

"There's no point in our working at cross purposes. You found out one of the niftiest capers ever set up. I have a lot of money. How would you like a piece of it?"

I had to play along with him. "I don't think so. I have more imagination than Cartwright."

He nodded in agreement.

"Ted was a wild talent, but not much imagination. What sort of a figure did you have in mind?"

Before I could answer, he spun around and picked up a slim leather case and unzipped the top. I saw a sheaf of engraved papers.

"These are the negotiable bonds. Twelve million will have to discounted, but ten million are bearer payable. I'm willing to give you twenty-five percent of what we realize."

"What do I have to do for that?"

"Come along with me. We'll be quite a couple in the sunny countries."

Motley had accepted without any display of feeling the capture of one of his crew. I didn't for a moment believe he was in earnest about the money, but if he thought he had my cooperation, he might relax his vigilance when we got out of these close quarters. I didn't want to give in too easily.

"One quarter of twenty million is nice, but how do I know I can keep it?"

For answer, he handed me the case.

"If we're caught, you're carrying it. In the meantime, you have a hundred percent of it. Money's so useful. It helps clear up people's thinking. If things don't work out for us, you can take your five million and I'll take the rest. How's that?"

"What's to stop you from taking the money away from me?"

He shook his head again.

"I thought you were smart, Susan. What's the difference between twenty-two million and seventeen million? I want money, but I'm not a miser. Makes sense, doesn't it?"

He was right. Figures that high aren't really money. He stared at me, as if he were watching my mind go round the problem and come up with his answer. After a moment, he seemed satisfied.

"OK. Let's go. Casanova Bliss will be arriving shortly, and I'd just as soon not be here when he does. It could create all sorts of problems—Davers in the inner office, Lawnover in the closet."

He didn't let me have my shoes.

While we walked to the president's car, he kept my thumb bent back against my wrist after giving it an educational twist to show what would happen if I tried to get away.

"Hurts, doesn't it?" he said. "You don't really trust me yet, so I don't trust you. But things are breaking for me, there's no moon tonight. I think you'll come along, too."

He shoved me through the driver's door into the front

seat and hit the power lock switches after we were in. Then he made me fasten my seat belts. "Safety first, sweetpants," he said.

We screamed out of the driveway, but once we were on the avenue leading to the freeway, he slowed down. I didn't know if I could override the locks and decided I couldn't chance it. There we were on the freeway and I'd lost my opportunity. I didn't know this section of town at all, but I could tell it was industrial development, empty at this hour.

Off to the north, I saw a small plane blinking navigation lights as it took off into the dark. Of course. Motley had another aircraft. He was willing to let Cartwright be caught while he took off with most of the loot. Inside an hour he'd be across state borders and within a day, he could be any place. By the time he could be traced, he'd be out of the country.

And I was with him.

I studied his face in the glow of the instruments on the dash. We were in the middle lane, doing fifty-seven miles an hour, and occasionally another car passed us. We were a man and a woman driving down a freeway. I was as alone as if stranded in the desert.

"Why did you kill all those people? Barker? Tate? Davers?"

He gave me a sidelong, humorous look.

"You have some kind of scenario where you ask the murderer what his plans were and then you escape to tell the police? I'll tell you. I was responsible for the ghendo seeds. I had to discredit you publicly because you were getting close. I had Cartwright drain your brakelines and I phoned the police anonymously. Bronterre vandalized your apartment. That business with Kenny was something Cartwright cooked up, but that's all."

He looked at me to see how I was taking the revelations.

"One other thing, but you'll find out about that soon enough. But murdering those academics—it wasn't necessary. Susan, that kind of accusation isn't worthy of you."

"I agree," I told him, "but as long as you're talking, you're not going to—what do you call it?—scarf me. You won't get away, you know."

He took a hand off the wheel to pat my knee and give my thigh a quick massage. It was all I could do to keep still.

"You still don't understand, little lady. I think you're a high number. I want to jump on your bones and listen to you talk. I don't know why you took such an unreasoning dislike to the old stud. What does it take to get your attention? I meant what I said. Five million is yours to come along quietly. When we get to where we're going, you can take your share and leave. You'll end up with a lot more money than your daddy has and it will be all tax free. In the meantime, we're friends—with all that implies."

I thought about the implications of what he said. My mind was spinning in circles. Now I believed him. He really wanted me and since the money was his bribe, he was certain he had me. I remembered the old joke about the millionaire who asked the woman if she'd go to bed with him for a million dollars. When she said yes, he offered her two dollars. Insulted, she asked him what he thought she was and got the answer that he knew what she was, he was trying to establish the price. After thinking it over for a while, I wondered if I could open the window and throw out the briefcase before Motley could stop me.

He patted my knee again as if he'd read my mind.

"I like women who think things over. How do you know the paper I showed you was real?"

Motley had nothing at all in common with Lawnover

or anyone else I'd met in this town except perhaps Harry Bliss. Both of them were steel under an apparently casual exterior. All this was clearly some kind of a test.

He started slowing the car and my heart speeded up. We were coming to a lighted barrier. Maybe I could do something. He gave me another sidelong look and slowed the car even more as we slid up to the immigration check but he didn't say anything. The man in the uniform of the Border Patrol looked us over and waved us on. We obviously weren't Mexican nationals. As we accelerated once more, Motley turned to me.

"Why didn't you shout for help?"

I smiled, feeling as if my face was going to give me away if I didn't.

"I thought you said I wasn't in danger," I told him, making an enormous effort of will and moving slightly toward him.

He patted my knee again and gave my thigh some more massage that ended with a painful tweak.

"You're not, and the Border Patrolman will remember that you didn't show any signs of wanting to escape. You're implicated now, my dear. Does that money seem a little more real to you?"

The money didn't, but the dimensions of my situation did. This man was a professional, and he had spent most of his life manipulating people in situations exactly like this. For the first time, I began to wonder if I would be able to get away from him.

"The money is real, but you're not. Cartwright was a member of your gang, you betrayed him to the police. Why should you treat me any differently?"

I had decided Motley was only interested in what he couldn't have. He took out a cigar and looked at me.

"Bite off the end, sweetcheeks. Cartwright let me down once when I was counting on him. Also, he's dumb. I kept him around to pay him off—with interest.

As you probably guessed, he was the turkey who kept all the academics watching the EC project while we stole the rest of Benson blind. Cartwright is a lesson for you. He crossed me and he's got thirty years ahead of him. You haven't let me down."

It all made sense. Cartwright had counted on Motley to protect him, so he did whatever he was told, no matter how senseless. I bit off the end of the cigar and handed it back to him as I pushed in the cigar lighter. Motley smiled and I felt dirty.

Ahead of us, I could see the beacon of another airfield, one that specialized in small planes. Motley apparently knew it quite well because we did not slow down at the entrance but took a turning around the main building and sped down a darkened side road where a number of small aircraft were parked. We drove for a long time and finally pulled up at a plane that had twin engines.

"All out for transfer to Mexico and points south," he said, pushing the unlock switch and getting out. I undid my seat belts and picked up the briefcase and got out myself. We were stopped behind the plane on a roadway that was paved with sharp gravel. I felt it against my soles immediately. Motley seemed to have thought of everything. I couldn't run very far or fast on that surface, and even if I could outdistance him, he'd catch me in the car before I could get anywhere.

"We'll wait in the plane," he said, taking my arm. "Your feet must be cold. It'll be warmer in the plane, my dear."

I looked up into the plane and saw a cigarette glow and then darken in the cabin.

"You seem to be having it all your way," I said. "Is that Bronterre?"

He chuckled as he undid the side door.

"No, but it's somebody you may remember."

He kept his hand on my arm, with his thumb and forefingers lightly around the tendons above my elbow. If I tried to jerk away, there would be a lot of pain and I wouldn't be successful. I smothered a sigh and made the long step up into the little cabin.

I recognized her face in the glow of her cigarette. I'd been expecting Gloria Keeney, but it was Naomi Wilson. She frowned when she saw me.

Eleven

The swelling on her lips had gone down and she looked herself again, and only a little shamefaced in the illumination from the landing strip lights off to the right of us.

"Get acquainted, ladies," Motley said. "You're going to be together a lot," he went on as he climbed into the pilot's seat after undoing the tie-downs. "I'll be busy here for a bit. Naomi, put out your cigarette and answer Susan's questions nicely. Tell her about Lester and Tatum."

Naomi looked at me defiantly. "After that trial and all that talk, you still didn't get me my job back. Then Roger came around like the Good Humor man. He showed me it was a merry-go-round with no ring for me. Then we got friendly. Since then, I been doing his bidding."

She gave me a look that was half-proud, half-shamed.

"He said all I had to do was let them mark me a little, and we'd be off to a warm island forever. Looks like it's working, doesn't it, Ms. Affirmative Action? I did everything I was supposed to for years and got nothing. Now I break rules and everything I want falls into my lap."

I could see her point, but she'd made a complete fool of me.

"So, it was all a put-up," I gritted at her. "If you're

here, he didn't get Daniel's unlisted phone number, you supplied it. Where's Gloria Keeney?"

"That turkey!" Naomi said. "She's laugh city, isn't she, Roger?"

"Whatever you say, my dear. Somebody had to get caught along with Cartwright," he said looking up from hitting switches. He turned around to pat her knee. He was some knee patter.

"Susan's qualifying for a piece of the loot too, Naomi," he said as he patted. That stopped all conversation for a bit. Naomi looked at me as if she had lost a friend—which she had. Motley started the engines one after another. The plane shook at first and then settled down to a steady vibration. When all the needles were pointing straight up, he killed the motors and took out a cigarro he didn't light but chewed on as if it were a blade of grass.

"We're waiting here for Bronterre. He's made other arrangements to transport his goodies," he said. "The next stop is Juarez. Naomi, no more smoking till we're airborne. Besides, smoking is bad for you, my dear."

"You are bad for me, Roger," she said, putting a hand on his neck and looking at me boldly. At first I wondered why she seemed so defensive, then I got it. Motley wanted a harem, and we were to be the core. Already Naomi was starting the age-old warfare about a man that has kept women enemies of each other for millennia. It was a game I'd never played and wasn't about to start now.

There was another problem that really troubled me. I don't like flying. In big jets, I tell myself I'm riding in a large bus, but in a plane as small as this, I am frightened to death. I know all about the theory of flight, but once airborne, all my logic deserts me. At every bump or lift I expect the wings to fall off. It's not the collision with the ground that frightens me, it's the falling sensation.

Daniel Derbyshire tried everything, even volunteering to pay for a course with a psychologist in California who claims a ninety percent cure rate. That seemed like relying on Daddy to get out of difficulties and I hadn't done it. Now I wished I had.

Motley glanced at his watch and turned around in his seat, for all the world like the captain of a jet reassuring passengers before a flight.

"Susan, I'm qualified as an instructor in all piston aircraft as well as a number of military jets, so you're in good hands. If Bronterre isn't here in five minutes he'll have to find another means of leaving the country. If he ran into trouble, we're leaving."

He turned around and chewed on his cigarro as Naomi leaned forward to whisper in his ear. I was going over and over my lack of options when we saw car lights round the end of the main building at the other side of the field. A small plane came in, silhouetted against the eerie blue lights of the landing path. The other car followed the road we had taken, turned off the paved lanes, and came down the gravel path that led to our plane. The other aircraft turned at the end of the runway and trundled back toward the main building. Motley pulled open the sliding window and I could hear the other plane's engine fanning quietly. The car coming toward us turned off its headlights and drove slower under parking lights only till it was about thirty feet off. Then the lights went out and the engine was killed. Someone honked the car's horn once, briefly.

"That's Bronterre," Motley said, "not a minute early, not a minute late." He put his head around to look at me. "You can see this is a class operation all the way."

I, and everyone else on the campus, had been made fools of by these people. I had prided myself on understanding academic types, but as Barry Martin had said, these men were pirates. Each of the three men had chosen an objective and all of them had reached it. Bronterre had obviously gutted the art collection, but he had done it in some way that had utterly misled Barry Martin.

Still sitting inside the car, Bronterre put a flashlight under his face. It was a strong flashlight and he flashed it on us before extinguishing it immediately.

Then two things happened.

All the lights on the field went out. The landing lights quenched, the lights in the main building were next, and finally, the beacon stopped rotating. When the beacon went out, Motley grabbed a handful of my hair and put something cold and metallic under my jaw.

He was holding me so my head was beside his, and I had an excellent view of what happened next. I heard the door of the car open. Then Bronterre got out followed by another man who stood close to him.

"It's no use, Roger," Bronterre said. "That bloody Bliss was everywhere tonight. He wants what you have."

The flashlight came into our eyes again and I decided that the man behind Bronterre was Stainfield. I was sure of it when he spoke.

"That's right, Motley. Everybody out."

Motley shoved me backward and dropped his pistol in his lap. Then he hit the ignition switch and after a whine, first one and then the other engine started to thrash and then settled into a steady throb. There would be no more conversation with Bronterre and Stainfield. Motley seemed unconcerned as he ran up the engines and began to turn the plane toward the runway that was at least a quarter of a mile off. He picked up the micro phone as if nothing had happened.

"Tower. This is Tango Foxtrot Four Four One, requesting permission to take off on runway one as per filed plan."

There was some cackling of static and then Bliss came on, loud and clear.

"Tango Foxtrot. Permission denied. The field is shut down as of now. You have a wanted suspect on board. Kill your engine and stand by for police search."

Motley said something under his breath but he kept the plane moving slowly across the uneven grass field toward the end of the runway. I was wondering about trying to interfere with his movements, but he had a pistol in his lap and I didn't know how I could stop him from doing anything for very long. Apparently, it occurred to him, too. He picked up the microphone again and looked at Naomi.

"Sweetcheeks, you make sure that little Miss AA there doesn't interfere."

And then he started talking into the microphone as if it were a woman he was seducing.

"Bliss, I have two hostages here. I want Bronterre released right now and you'll get one in return. The other is going with us, but we'll turn her loose when we get where we're going. You have ten seconds to make a deal."

Immediately a car screamed around the corner of the main building and pulled up at the other end of the air strip that was still a couple of hundred yards away from us.

"Give it up, Motley. He can block your take off."

"One of the hostages is Susan Meredith, Romeo. How do you like that? That other is an ethnic lady. You don't want bad headlines, do you?"

With no hesitation at all, the voice came back, but it didn't sound like Harry.

"I know. She's the one I want. I have a warrant for the arrest of Susan Meredith for the murders of Barker and Tate."

Naomi sucked in her breath audibly. Even Motley seemed startled. He looked at me with an enigmatic smile. I decided that Harry was something else. The next time I had a crisis, I wanted to have him manage it for me. He'd turn me loose and then the police could stop the plane. Harry spoke again.

"Motley, I don't have anything on you, but I'm not going to let you take off with that woman on board."

Motley stared at the far end of the runway where the car had stopped, its headlights on high beam.

"All right," he said as if the mike were an ear he was whispering into, "we can make a deal. I'm taking off after the exchange. Get that car off the runway. You do it right now or these ladies are going to be dead ladies right away."

"Like the women at Kuchine, Motley?"

Motley's head jerked to one side. "You heard what I said," he grated. "Get it off. I'll let one of them loose. Then Bronterre gets aboard. You turn on the field lights and I let the other one off. And it's bye-bye."

"Negative, Motley. Both women out of the plane before Bronterre gets on."

Motley's voice was as relaxed as if he were about to go to sleep.

"I can't buy that. Move the car and send Bronterre over. As proof of my good will, I'll drop one of the women out when I see the runway clear and Bronterre on his way."

Harry's voice didn't come on again immediately, but the car at the other end of the driveway revved up and turned around to vanish as rapidly as it had come. Motley looked back at us. Naomi had been holding my arm and I hadn't even noticed it.

"We're down to the short strokes now. ladies, and

the tension mounts. OK. Naomi, you go out first."

Naomi looked as if he'd just punched her in the stomach.

"No, Roger. Make her get out. You and me, we go together."

Motley seemed to be only half listening as he craned his neck to look back where we had left Bronterre. Only when he saw a jouncing light that Bronterre held alternately on his face and on the ground ahead of him as he ran toward us, did he turn back to face her.

"Look, sweetlips, all they think you are is a hostage. Remember, you have that Diane Stronglady's evidence you've been kidnapped. I'll get in touch with you after we have everything taken care of. I need this lady as the second one out. Next thing you know, we'll be on our own Riviera, the way you always wanted."

I didn't spend any time thinking about how Naomi would take the news because it spelled death for me. But it worked for Naomi. She threw her arms around his neck and gave him a kiss that was supposed to last him till they met again. It was quite a picture, but I decided she had kissed him for the last time.

He braked the plane and opened the copilot's door.

"See you, sweetcheeks," he said. "Run toward the office building, and stay off the runway."

There was a certain amount of confusion as Naomi crawled over my legs and through the tight quarters of the fold-down seat beside the pilot. The lack of light didn't help much either, but finally, with one long soul look for Roger, she managed to leave the plane. Over her shoulder, I saw the slashing light that marked Bronterre's progress toward us. She began to run toward the office building. Motley turned to me.

"I guess you don't want to get out now. I've never had a lady who killed people she didn't like before. I'll have to stay on your good side."

Bronterre was still almost a football field off. Motley took a look at the instruments and then the runway. His lips writhed.

"Who were the women of Kuchine, Roger?" I asked.

"A rumor," he said. "I got my pension anyway. What about it? Do we wait for Bronterre? He's not making much speed and that dumb cop may change his mind. How about it?"

"My God!" I shouted. "Roger, the money! Naomi took it! Let me get her!"

I slid over the front seat like an eel and fell out of the door onto the runway on my elbows and knees, but I had the briefcase. I landed scrabbling for traction. I got to my feet as if I'd been fired out of a gun and then the lights all came on as if I were on a stage and caught in a spotlight.

I didn't wait for applause. I ran.

I ran across the gravel. Then rough grasses were stinging my ankles like fire, but I ran. I heard a shot behind me but now I was in the dark, running toward Bronterre.

We passed each other as if we were commuters running for trains. He didn't give me a glance. I kept on toward the car that Stainfield had brought Bronterre in. Behind me I heard a power roar but I didn't look back. Car headlights came alive in front of me and started moving toward me. I wasn't aware of my feet as anything but fire. The car lights came to me and I ran up to the driver's side door.

"Sergeant Stainfield! I have the money."

Stainfield got out, but he was looking past me, and I turned to watch Motley's escape.

He was moving down the runway now, but the beacon light, a shaft of white that I had thought was a spotlight, kept the plane's windshield targeted. The plane moved slower and slower, till it got almost halfway down the runway and came to a stop. Then I saw Naomi running for it. In a moment, she was pulled aboard. I could see her teeth flashing. Suddenly the plane spun around and came back the way it had been going and sped up. Now Motley didn't have the beacon destroying his night vision.

Not very gently, Stainfield pushed me into the police car. This had not been my night for chivalric behavior from men.

He keyed the engine and we roared across the grasses with everything going, lights, horn, PA microphone. He was going to try to block the plane at this end. We almost made it. Certainly, Motley took off sooner than he had intended because we skidded to a halt in the middle of the cement and I heard a thump as a wheel ticked our roof.

Then Stainfield was out of the car looking at the plane. I got out too, just in time to see the plane make a turn and then stop in mid-air. It had caught in some high tension wires. It exploded.

It burned like a kite. In the light of the flames, Stainfield's face was like stone. He turned and took my arm.

I'd been handled enough tonight.

"That's all right," I said mechanically, starting to shrug away. "He was going to kill me."

Stainfield looked at me with an odd expression. Then he put a handcuff on the wrist he was holding.

"Since when does murder trouble you?" he asked.

Stainfield had read me my rights and we were halfway back to town before I decided that Stainfield wasn't acting. But I still had flashes of him coming on strong with Tatum and Lester. Then I wondered if he'd been acting when he'd been so pleasant to me after Barker's murder. I stared out into the darkness. The world outside the academy was a lot more complicated than I had thought. Anyway, Harry was going to be Lieutenant Bliss till this got straightened out.

When Stainfield turned onto the metropolitan freeway, he picked up the microphone and said some numbers into it. Immediately, as if someone had been waiting for his call, an answer came back, also in code. The only words I understood were "crime site." We took the next exit and within minutes we were rolling through the main gates onto the campus.

"Why aren't we going to the station, if I'm under arrest?" I asked, surely a sensible question. Stainfield frowned but didn't take his eyes off the roadway where cars hemmed us in on both sides.

"You're a capital felony suspect in transport. Saying nothing is the best thing for you to do."

Finally, I felt arrested. I'd have to demand a lawyer. Bob Mercer would think I was mad for his body, but he was the only lawyer I knew.

We pulled into a No Parking space in front of the administration building where a couple of other official cars had double-parked. Stainfield got out and came around to help me. It wasn't chivalry. He'd fastened one handcuff to the grab bar on the door. He picked up the briefcase with that unbelievable amount of money as if it were a sack lunch and led me up the stairs to the presidential suite. When we got inside the foyer, he unlocked the other cuff and looked significantly at a young policeman.

"She doesn't go anyplace. Not even the john, right?"

Before the policeman had time to nod, Stainfield was through the door to the president's office and gone. I was still in my stocking feet and I felt as if I'd run over an acre of used razor blades. Now I was seeing what life was like when the police didn't like you. Then I wondered if Harry had been putting me on right along.

It wasn't fair, I decided. If I hadn't behaved like a good citizen, Motley would have gotten away with most of Benson's endowment fund. If I'd been guilty of anything, I'd have gone off with him. There would have been plenty of time to take off—and he'd asked me while Bronterre was running toward us. Of course, I'd have been with Roger Motley, which in the long run, wouldn't be much fun for a girl.

I sat in the reception area with the young policeman for quite a while. Other policemen came in and out with cameras and anonymous kits, but Bliss was nowhere in sight. Finally, Arnold Lawnover came out of the presidential office looking pale. A detective I hadn't met before brought him out and sat him down in a deep chair across from me. He looked at me briefly, but we didn't have anything to say to each other, so he sank back into his own thoughts. They could not have been pleasant because he was taken by fits of trembling now and again. I wondered how I could ever have thought he was my attacker. He seemed about as aggressive as a neurotic bunny cottontail. I kept waiting for Bliss to appear and say "Hold it!" and make everything all right. Stop it, I told myself. You can't have a crush on a man who allows you to be arrested.

Then Barry Martin came in, accompanied by Harvey Welles, the trustee in charge of the endowment fund, and another policeman I didn't recognize. As usual, Barry was talking, his long blond hair swinging as he walked. I saw that he was wearing a fur-lined raincoat. He had panache, that man.

"Of course, once I saw what was happening, I had to stop it, and I did—the only way I knew. Unfortunately, I was raised in a home that didn't even countenance war toys—and that was long before Viet Nam—so I sat down on him."

That was a fascinating bit of conversation, but I

didn't discover what it meant for some time because the detective ushered them right into the president's office, leaving me alone with Lawnover and the policeman. Then the outer door opened and Diane Sampson came in, also escorted by a policeman, this one in uniform.

"Well, helloo," she said, looking at me and Lawnover. "You had some excitement, didn't you, Sue-person?" Then she sighed. "It was too bad that Naomi turned out wrong. We were all set to get justice for that foxy lady. Well, they got Cartwright with almost a third of a million in vouchers and no explanation to go with them. Not bad, hey? Now maybe life will simmer down here for a while."

I nodded agreement, but I didn't want to tell Diane I was in trouble till I had a better idea of what the trouble was.

Before I could say anything, Barry Martin came out of the inner office with Harvey Welles, followed by Stainfield. Stainfield clapped Welles on the shoulder and nudged Barry into a chair. Welles left, carrying the briefcase with the young policeman who had been watching us as his escort. Stainfield stared at each of us in turn. I wondered where Harry Bliss was.

Twelve

At this point, the reception area for Benson's president looked like the waiting room of a dentist who specialized in root canal work. Barry was no longer ebullient. Diane's face was so stretched into tiredness that she looked almost plain. Lawnover seemed as made out of dough as he usually did, and I was still barefoot.

Then I saw that Stainfield had my shoes in his hand. He gave them to me and watched while I slipped them on. If anything, they made my feet hurt more, but at least I didn't feel like a juvenile among adults anymore. Stainfield pored over a sheaf of notes in silence while the rest of us watched each other. Nobody said anything, and I could feel the tension mounting. But nothing happened.

Just as we all began to relax, the door opened and a policewoman came in. Like Stainfield, she looked vaguely parental—about forty-five, somebody's cookie-making aunt. She stopped smiling when she saw Diane and me. Shrugging out of her uniform coat, she opened a briefcase on Mrs. Scott's desk and took out a portable taping system. After she propped up a microphone, she nodded at Stainfield. He sucked in his cheeks and stared at us collectively for a while. This suspense building takes time, I thought. When he spoke, I wished he'd taken longer.

"Susan Meredith is in custody on suspicion of

homicide. She murdered three people—Harrison Barker, Charles Benson Tate, and Marvin Davers. Her rights have been explained to her and we have you people here to help with the interrogation because you are, we believe, in possession of facts that will help us establish her guilt."

All three stared at me as if I'd been accused of committing a minor but gross social error. Barry Martin looked unbelieving. Diane's face was a mask, and Lawnover chewed his lips and stared at me. Three centuries ago he would have been burning witches.

"I didn't kill anyone," I said. "You police came into this case convinced that a woman or an ethnic killed Barker and nothing since has changed your minds. I didn't kill anyone. Attempts were constantly being made on my life."

The policewoman made a noise, which I thought was a comment, but when I glanced at her, she was blowing her nose into a kleenex. No sisterhood there. Stainfield put his notes down and didn't look at them again.

"Let's talk about those attempts. You claimed Mr. Lawnover attacked you on that Saturday night, but he was out of town."

"Somebody did," I said positively.

Stainfield lifted his lip to show his front teeth.

"I know you convinced the campus police and the lieutenant, but you didn't convince me, lady. I went over the scene. That fire door takes thirty-three seconds to slam closed. You ran back to the place the watchman found you and that was that."

I felt as if I'd touched an electric current.

"The bump on my head! What about the vandalizing of my apartment. What about that!"

Stainfield wasn't having any. "I'm not Bliss, Ms. Meredith. None of those things impressed me. There were no witnesses for the vandalizing. I think you tore up your apartment yourself. Your story about people attacking you was to cover you when you did your killing."

"What possible motive did I have?" I asked. "I'm new here. I scarcely knew these people."

Stainfield ignored my remark and looked at our audience as if he had to convince them. Except for Lawnover, they still looked neutral. He went on.

"As the Affirmative Action officer, you were unhappy with each of the three men who were Benson's presidents. You thought you could do a better job than any of them. Your motive was doctrinaire. You want to stamp out racism and sexism. Right?"

I could see why he'd studied the notes as if memorizing them. That's exactly what he'd been doing. He'd put in two questions, each demanding a different answer. If I wasn't careful, he'd have a recording saying I thought I'd be a better president or I didn't care about sexism. Stainfield had dimensions of subtlety I hadn't expected—unless Bliss had given him the wording. I wasn't going to answer with any monosyllables. Where was Lieutenant Harry Bliss?

"I had no opinion on how they did their jobs. I disagreed with their judgments on the Wilson case. But the disagreement wasn't a motive for murder, no matter what you say."

Stainfield acted as if I hadn't spoken.

"You're a healthy young woman. All three men were killed from behind by a weapon on the scene that you could have handled. Right?"

"I don't have to agree with anything you say. Being healthy doesn't make me a murderer. They could have been killed by an unhealthy male," I said with a look at Lawnover. He blanched and I liked that. But Stainfield stared at me with eyes that weren't really seeing me.

"You cannot account for your whereabouts immediately prior to any of those murders. Right?"

Despite everything, I suddenly began to shake with repressed fury and fright. He was trying to make me agree that I was a murderer!

"Ms. Meredith, you had the means, the motive, and the opportunity to kill all three of these men. Come on, you stupid broad, confess!" he suddenly shouted, slamming his notes down the way he'd swung the black jack in jail.

I can't take bullying from anyone. I was frightened no longer. I was angry, and the angrier I get, the closer I am to having water come out of my eyes, and that makes me angrier still.

"Sergeant Stainfield!" I said in my Nancy Chambers voice. "You have asked me questions and not listened to my answers. Let me ask you some. First. While I was supposed to be murdering Dr. Barker, someone was attempting to kill me. The truck on the ramp, or don't you remember?"

Stainfield didn't have to consult his notes.

"All you had to do was release the brakes on a physical plant truck that was parked at the top of an incline. Then you could say it almost ran you down. You could do that after you killed Barker. His hand falling on the phone buzzer was consistent with rigor mortis. Remember, you were the one who hung up the phone. That would explain any fingerprint smudges you might have left. For a woman who'd supposedly had a brush with death, you seemed very composed. That was the first thing that made me suspect you."

It made a kind of fit. Stainfield went on like a telephone solicitor who pays no attention to what you say but keeps to his catechism.

"Any of you people have any evidence to offer that gives this broad an alibi?"

Barry Martin was looking sympathetic, Diane was blank, and so was Lawnover.

"Then let's go on to Dr. Tate. He was struck with a weapon right between the shoulder blades. It crushed a vertebra and he was dead by the time he hit the bottom of the stairs. I think you had an argument in his office. You followed him out the door and jabbed him in the back. Then you ran over to the trustee meeting and waited to hear about it."

"I talked to him on the phone," I said with a sinking feeling. All my evidence was unwitnessed. "We came to an agreement about the Wilson case. Dr. Davers had the argument with Dr. Tate."

Doubt was painted on every face, including Diane's.

"You can ask Mrs. Scott," I said. Then I remembered that Tate had phoned me.

Stainfield curled his lips in scorn.

"Davers is dead and Mrs. Scott was having a late lunch. Tate had dictated some notes for the board meeting during her regular hour. All your alibis are made out of your unsupported word."

When Stainfield said this, I calmed down immediately. The scrap of paper in Tate's hand bore out my story that he'd changed his mind, but I was still interested in what was torn off that piece of paper.

"Let's talk about motives, Sergeant," I said, looking around the room. "There are all sorts of motives to kill people on this campus. Stronger than mine could be. Harriet Guyon could have killed Barker for a number of crimes from popping gum in committee meetings to trying to destroy her career. Look at Dr. Martin. He was convinced the administration was ready to sell off the art collection to increase the endowment. That's a motive, isn't it, Barry?"

He gave me a smile that helped a lot. "That's true, Susan. Of course I'd kill anybody who'd try to peddle a collection that took decades to assemble. But tonight when I caught Bronterre and that Gallic excrescence exchanging replicas for our pieces, I merely sat on them and called the police. If I'd known how, I'd have killed them. As it is, they'll only do jail time."

Stainfield broke in to stare at the rest of them. "Bronterre's dead. We think this broad sabotaged the airplane. It took out Motley and that Wilson broad, too."

I'm a slow learner, but Stainfield finally communicated to me. I was much more poised when I went on.

I turned to Diane. "Diane, you're stronger than I am, stronger than most men. These people were exploiting the Education Continuation project. You knew it was going to hurt Dr. Henderson in the long run. Even though he wasn't connected with it, it had been his proposal. If you thought someone was trying to harm him, you'd kill them, wouldn't you?"

Diane's face lit up as she nodded me a strong affirmative and smiled at Stainfield.

"Sue-person is right. Anybody messes with my main man and I kill them. Then I cook them up for soup and not think on it one more time."

She sighed. "But Stainfield is trying to fit you for that suit. You say you didn't. It's good enough for me."

Before I could turn to Arnold Lawnover, he jumped to his feet and began to talk.

"I have a statement to make," he informed the room at large. "Before Susan Meredith can make any baseless accusations about me, I want to go on record with some information that is vital."

He whipped off his aviator glasses and polished them with his breast handkerchief. I remembered our first encounter and his "matter of considerable consequence." He was a turkey in tweed!

"I know nothing of the murders of Barker or Tate.

As you know, Sergeant, I was out of town for the first and I was at the trustees meeting before Susan Meredith arrived—as she may well tell you. But this evening, when Dr. Davers did not arrive for a meeting with Bronterre and Dr. Martin and myself, I went over to his office. There I found Ms. Meredith in the office with Dr. Davers dead. I told Lieutenant Bliss, but I don't think you know it."

Well! That's why Stainfield was conducting this interrogation. Bliss thought I was the guilty one. All right for him. It was up to me to prove I was innocent.

But Arnold Lawnover was giving testimony like a teacher's pet offering the answer no one else knew. He looked at me and I knew he thought he was going to pay off every thought I'd ever had about him.

"She appeared to be sticking Dr. Davers with a spear from off the wall. Certainly, Dr. Davers was dead, but in all fairness I must say that I didn't hear any cry."

Lawnover was a fool, but he had a certain low cunning, I decided. He was underplaying it. He went on, an incipient wince in his posture as if I were going to explode, but I had no such plan.

"She said she was trying to take the spear out, but it does follow the pattern you pointed out earlier—a weapon from the scene, a blow from behind, a piece from behind, a piece of sculpture, a window pole, and now a spear."

Lawnover's voice went on relentlessly. "Then Motley arrived and I assumed that Motley had killed Davers, even though he said he hadn't. When he shut me into the closet and shot out the light, I thought he had killed me and I fainted."

He looked around the room to see how this was going down. He should have been happy. Stainfield looked cheery. Martin was staring at me neutrally, and Diane looked sad. The policewoman was examining her machine. Lawnover took a deep breath.

"I have a confession to make, Sergeant. It was something I didn't tell the lieutenant. I came on the scene just seconds after Ms. Meredith killed Dr. Tate, I am convinced."

Stainfield made a welcoming gesture to Lawnover.

"We need every bit of evidence we can get, Doc. Did you actually see her with the window pole in her hands?"

Lawnover answered right up.

"I was on my way over to the meeting and I apparently came around the corner at the instant that she killed him, because I'd heard a groan and the sound of a body falling down the stairs. I saw the window pole vanish around the corner and I heard a woman's footsteps—you know, high heels—running away. Then an outside door banged."

Stainfield was instantly grave.

"Why didn't you tell us about this before, Doc?"

Teacher's pet was ready. "Well, I knew that this woman was a very close friend of Lieutenant Bliss's and he'd already, on her say so, tried to put me at the scene of the crime in Dr. Barker's murder. I didn't want that to happen again. This time I didn't have a perfect alibi. So I went over to the trustee's meeting. She must have been hiding the window pole someplace because she came in after I did."

Stainfield turned his heavy face toward me. Barry Martin stood up and looked compassionate.

"Susan, I don't know what to make of this, but I think you should refuse to say anything without a lawyer present."

Stainfield said something I didn't catch, but it made Barry's face turn white. Just then the corridor slammed open and Harry—Lieutenant Bliss, I corrected myself—came through in a hurry.

"Sit down, Diane! You, too, Barry! Stainfield, I told you to keep the lid on till I got back. What in hell have you been doing?"

Stainfield's snarl was worse than anything I'd seen him use on Lester and Tatum.

"Breaking this case open, College Boy! I got your shack job lined up for the DA. That's what. I have the warrant and all. I been doing policework, not screwing around over in the courthouse."

Bliss looked as if Stainfield and all the rest of us had deeply disappointed him.

"Keep that up, Stan, and you'll be a traffic patrolman in front of an elementary school." He looked around the room. "These cases have been pretty complicated because there were two activities going on, murder and embezzlement. The embezzlement has been straightened out, and all the criminals are dead or in jail. Now all we have is the murder problem. And that shouldn't cause us any difficulty."

He looked at Stainfield.

"Cuff her and read her her rights, Stan," he said, pointing at Diane.

When Bliss said that, I decided I could never forgive him. He'd put me through that wringer and hadn't given me any warning. Then I was on my feet, shouting "No!"

But Lawnover was shaking his head and glaring at me as he yelled something incomprehensible and thrust an arm in my direction. "*No*," he finally brought out. "It was that Meredith woman! She was wearing high heels. I caught just a flash of her going out the door."

Through all this, Diane sat as calm as a queen while peasants rioted in a distant province.

Bliss frowned.

"You mean you actually saw Susan Meredith with the pole in her hand? You're certain? You'll have to stand up to defense questioning, Arnold."

Arnold put on a superb look.

"I was almost certain, but not enough. Then when you were going to arrest an innocent person, something flashed in my memory and I saw her as clear as could be. I'm sorry I didn't recall it before. The human mind, you know, is a strange organ."

"I'm sorry you didn't too, Arnold. Dr. Davers would be alive today if you had." He turned to me. "Sue, how many pairs of high-heeled shoes do you have?"

"One," I said, "black patent leathers I wear for dress."

Harry looked glumly back at Lawnover.

"Too bad, Arnold. She wasn't wearing high-heeled shoes when Tate got it. No, it's still Diane."

I decided this had gone on long enough.

"Hold it, Lieutenant," I said as if I'd coined a phrase. "If we look at Mrs. Scott's notes, we'll find what was torn off that page Tate had in his hand. I'll bet it was a recommendation that Arnold Lawnover be fired as presidential assistant."

That shut everything down. It was a gamble, but Lawnover suddenly giggled. Then I was sure.

"The big problem has been his alibi for Barker's murder. I figured it out just now. His secretary is his sister. She stayed the night in Sun City while Arnold caught the last flight in. He killed Barker because he knew Barker didn't want any off campus publicity about the project."

Lawnover stood so stiffly he almost vibrated. His voice came through tight jaws.

"You. Are. A. Loose. Woman."

He'd made the calls.

"I know this because your wife told me, Arnie. Just

before she got in touch with a divorce lawyer. She hates you and your sister and the way you've treated her, Arnie."

Quicker than I could have thought, Lawnover swept a tall bronze table lamp off Mrs. Scott's desk and was swinging it at me. Even before I could flinch, Bliss had stepped between us and caught the lamp in mid-swing. It stopped as if it were painted in the air.

"All *right!*" he said, twisting the heavy lamp out of Lawnover's hands. "Show and tell time."

He pushed Lawnover into a chair.

"Stan, talk to the man," he said as he turned to the rest of us.

"Sorry about all the play acting, but we had to break Lawnover open, and I had to have women and minorities to do it. He feels so inferior that he needs to identify with authority. That's why I wanted two women and you, Barry, right here."

Barry began to laugh. Then Diane, but I didn't.

Diane and Barry left together after lots of hugs and head shakings. I was still mad. Bliss had explained their roles to Barry and Diane, but not to me.

Stainfield arrested Lawnover and then took him and the female police officer into the inner office where the murders had taken place. Even as we talked, I could hear Stainfield hammering away at Arnold as if he were driving tentstakes, asking question after question and not letting him answer. Suddenly, Arnold began to answer. I heard his voice begin as if he were addressing a large audience.

"Everything I have done, I have done for Benson."

I decided I didn't want to listen any more. Bliss was still in trouble with me, I remembered, but it was hard to recall, hearing him explain in a low voice that still sent shivers through me, his bedroom voice.

"Lawnover is a classic type. Tightly compensated, he has to be totally in charge of his domestic life before he can function at all in society. I was pretty sure you were the focus of his apprehensions, so I had Stan play against you first. If that didn't work, to go for Barry or Diane, but Lawnover wasn't troubled about blacks or gays, it was the independent woman that really rattled his cage."

I was about to ask why I hadn't been prepped, but Bliss tucked me even deeper under his arm. Typical masterful male, I told myself comfortably. It's OK as long as he doesn't do anything I seriously disagree with.

"When you suggested his wife had proclaimed her independence, everything he feared about you came true. You came on this campus for the express purpose of destroying his life, he thought. That's why I was at the courthouse while Stainfield was working you over. Lawnover owned that house in common with his sister, who was also his secretary. She was a lot more important to him than his wife ever had been."

"How did you find that out?"

"Police procedure," he told me in a grandiose way. "Do you think I'd take long distance word that he'd been down in Sun City with a perfect alibi? You forget I didn't like him either. The witnesses down there saw his secretary but not him the next morning. We checked the passenger list on the last commuter flight up here and accounted for everybody except a Mr. Smith who sounded an awful lot like Lawnover. Then I went to talk to his wife."

He gave me that smile again.

"She told me everything, but she didn't understand much that was going on. She overheard the phone call to you, and Lawnover went out after that. When he came back, his clothes were ruined and he smelled funny. I discharged a fire extinguisher and she recognized the smell.

"Then why did you have to put me through that wringer with Stainfield?"

He squeezed me under his arm again. It was like taking shelter under a large spreading tree during a rainstorm, calm, quiet, and cozy. I could learn to like that.

"How many members of the middle class have been executed for murder in this country in the last decade?"

He didn't wait for my answer.

"None. Unless we could break him down publicly the way we did, there was no way our other evidence would stand up. His wife couldn't testify against him. His alibi for Sun City is debatable. But we got it all on tape. You remember I told you Tate had been killed by a window pole? I didn't tell anyone else. But Lawnover knew it and he had to say, after Stainfield teed you up that he could place you there. When he did that, he demonstrated guilty knowledge."

"If you knew all these things, why didn't you tell him instead of running me through that questioning from Stainfield? He's frightening when he starts."

"I had everything on him certain in my own mind," Harry said comfortably, "but I didn't have anyplace to push him until he made that admission. I was certain he'd attacked you that Saturday night because he's physically ineffective. He hid in a storeroom Monday morning. When he saw you coming, he started that truck rolling at you and hid again. Then he remembered about the nine o'clock appointment, and he skipped into Barker's office and dropped his hand onto the buzzer, stepping out the hall door. Then he had only half an hour until his sister arrived from Sun City and he was home free. But, his alibi was just barely good enough."

I had a lot of questions, but I wondered how he managed to kill people when I didn't have an alibi so often.

"How could he be sure about my whereabouts before Tate was killed?"

"He wasn't, I decided. You're an executive, your time is at your own disposal. He killed Tate, who was going to fire him anyway—as Mrs. Scott's shorthand notes prove—and he went back into the president's office. Since Mrs. Scott was out to lunch, he could walk into his own office from there and his sister wasn't going to inform on him."

Harry saw my next question shaping on my face.

"He lost it tonight. We had him followed constantly. He came over here ostensibly to get Davers, but really to kill him. He was going to say he found him dead, but just after he'd speared him, he heard you coming. Like the rest, he came up behind him."

I had one more question, and I came out from under the oak tree to ask it.

"Why didn't you do me the same courtesy you did Diane and Barry Martin? You were treating me like a silly piece of fluff, not letting me in on the secret."

He was studying my face moonily. His expression didn't change.

"The same reason I had Stan ask you all those mean questions. I couldn't do it with a straight face, and I didn't think you'd give the right answers if you weren't angry. And I wanted you mad at Stanfield, not me. Not even for a second mad at me. I figured you would catch on about halfway through. You did, didn't you?"

I had, but I didn't intend to let him off the hook. For a few minutes, till Stainfield had accused me of sabotaging Motley's plane, I'd been worried.

"Did you ever think I might have been the murderer? Stainfield was making a pretty good case."

Harry yawned at me.

"My dear, there's only one way you could kill a man."

I was about to ask him what *that* meant, when he turned to shout in the door to the president's office.

"We're going home, Stan. Finish up!"